Souvenirs from Mar del Plata

Praise for *Marina Caamaño*

"The plot of *Souvenirs from Mar del Plata* is straight-foward and easily relatable: four women take a vacation together but have trouble getting along. But it is Caamaño's ability to create obsessive characters that makes her writing so fun to read. We *believe* their obsessions, then we become obsessed as well, in a rush to turn the pages, then sad when we've finished. Great story."

Billy McCall,
author of *Chicago Joe and the Ancient Pages*

"With a screenplay-like precision... and a sharp balance between dialogue and interior monologue, *Souvenirs from Mar del Plata* might be a literary, female, and distinctly Argentine take on *The Hangover*."

Juliana Rodríguez,
La Voz del Interior

"Being human can be awkward, painful, and humiliating. This book captures that particular trinity of shit in hilarious fashion. Hands down one of the funniest people I've ever met, Marina Caamaño is a bad-ass, wild international treasure. This is Fear and Loathing in Argentina."

Adam Gnade,
author of *After Tonight, Everything Will Be Different*

"I laughed so hard I had to put the book down to take deep, calming breaths. Marina Caamaño is one of my favorite contemporary writers."

Nathaniel Kennon Perkins,
author of *Wallop*

"Marina Caamaño doesn't just write—she surfs. Her prose has the freshness and ease of the waves, diving into the absurdity of reality to reveal its most ridiculous and hilarious side. In that liminal space where literature rarely lingers, she uncovers small gems that turn the mundane into something dazzling. *Souvenirs from Mar del Plata* glides gracefully between tenderness and irony—Caamaño's unmistakable signature."

Mat Guillan,
author of *What You Don't Expect from Me*

"Caamaño develops her characters skillfully, with almost no description, moving swiftly from one action to the next, from event to event. This is a book that can be read in a single sitting, in an afternoon—it could easily be adapted into a screenplay, brought to the big screen, and who knows, maybe even make it to the Mar del Plata Film Festival."

Milagros Carnevale,
Agencia Paco Urondo

Originally published in Spanish as *Recuerdos de Mar del Plata* by Caballo Negro Editora (Argentina) in 2020

Translation copyright © 2025 Marina Caamaño & Nathaniel Kennon Perkins

Without limiting the rights under copyright, no part of this publication may be reproduced, stored in or introduced into a retrieval system, or transmitted, in any form or by any means (electronic, mechanical, photocopying, recording, or otherwise), without the prior written permission of both the copyright owner and the publisher of this book.

ISBN: 978-1-951226-220

Cover illustration by María Ortiz Byrne

Published by Trident Press
940 Pearl St.
Boulder, CO 80302

tridentcafe.com/trident-press-titles

SOUVENIRS FROM MAR DEL PLATA

by Marina Caamaño

Trident Press
Boulder, CO

I was in the park running and listening to music and thinking about several things at once, my thoughts all jumbled together, when I felt a hand on my back. The sun had gone down and it was drizzling. Other than the two or three other people I'd run past, there wasn't really anyone around. The image of a huge man with a stick or a gun flashed in my mind. I was scared, but I didn't really react. I kept running at the same pace and turned my head slightly, afraid of what I might see. But it was just some guy. He was wearing black running shorts, a black t-shirt, and a black baseball cap. He smiled and waved. His lips were moving, but because my music was turned up so loud I couldn't hear anything he was saying. I was sure I knew him from somewhere, but I couldn't quite place him. It wasn't uncommon for me to fail to recognize people on the street, either because I was lost in thought or because I wasn't wearing my glasses, without which I couldn't distinguish anything more than blurred shapes. Sometimes, like now, it was because of both things at the same time. I smiled and raised my hand to wave back anyway. He ran faster than I did. I stared after him as he disappeared into the darkness. Between the shadows and the amber reflections of the dim park lights, he seemed to become a galloping black horse. I slowed down, trying to put a name to the face, which was like playing a mental slot machine: on one side was his picture, fixed in place, while on the other were several quickly spinning images of people I knew. I felt the gambler's adrenaline. I might hit the jackpot any second. But there was never a match. I lost focus and stopped running.

On my way home, it started raining harder, so I went into a gas station to wait it out. I got a bottle of water and a pack of cigarettes, and I sat at one of the inside tables by the windows that looked out at the pumps. A group of teenage girls entered the shop, each wearing a backpack and each with a cell phone in hand. They shouted, laughing at their wet hair and taking selfies. I put my headphones back on so I wouldn't have to hear them as they disappeared into the aisles of chips and cookies. Outside, a group of cyclists gathered under the roof that covered the gas pumps. They looked each other over, as if the rain had somehow damaged their clothes and professional-level bikes. They leaned over each other, then squatted, feeling their torsos, stretching their arms, their legs. Their movements seemed meticulously choreographed in perfect sync with the song I was listening to, as if they were appearing in the music video, dancing behind the lead singer with their helmets, knee pads, and fingerless gloves, dripping, a torrent of rain falling behind them. I continued to stare through the rapidly fogging windows until, out of nowhere, the guy from the park appeared once more, soaking wet. From outside, he hit the window right in front of my face. He held a half-liter blue Gatorade in his other hand. He entered the gas station and sat across from me.

The first part of the conversation was a little awkward. While we were going through the *how-are-yous* and the *everything-okays* and started talking about the weather, my brain began playing the slot machine game again, but this time the images were spinning even faster. My desperate mind was searching for a match, unable to pay attention to anything else that was going on. The gas station became a silent world. Then one of the teenagers turned her wallet upside down. The noise of the coins bouncing on the ceramic floor triggered a sensation of pleasure in my mind, forcing me to close my eyes for a few moments. When I opened them again, there was no doubt: the guy in black shorts and a cap was the Thrush. The night I'd met him, we'd been at a party and he'd diluted LSD in a pitcher of Campari and orange juice. It wasn't until everyone had drunk it that he confessed we'd been dosed. Almost everyone laughed, but the hostess got super angry and kicked us all out. Instead of blaming the Thrush, we ended up at another party at the nearby house of one of his friends. That had been a great night.

The Thrush couldn't understand why, after running, I would drink plain water instead of Gatorade. Plus, I was a smoker. I told him that the blue liquid tasted like disgusting salty sweat to me. As for the cigarettes, they didn't interfere with my workout in any way. While he began preaching against tobacco companies and in defense of the sport drink's hydrating properties, Romina, a friend I'd met in a photography workshop, popped into my mind. She was another person who tended to lecture me about my smoking habit, despite bumming one cigarette after another off me every time we went out together. I also remembered that she'd once told me she wanted to try acid. I didn't really know anyone who could get acid. Whenever I did manage to get it, it was from a friend of a friend of a friend that knew someone, but it was easy to lose contact with those kinds of people, so I took advantage of my encounter with the Thrush to address the topic.

"Can you get me some acid?" I asked quite directly, interrupting his speech on how smoking decreased my lung capacity and endurance when running.

The Thrush opened his black eyes wide, leaned back in his chair, and placed one hand (the hand that wasn't holding the blue Gatorade he wouldn't let go of) on the table.

He looked serious and said, "I mean, it's not an easy thing to get, you know, but I think we can probably work something out."

He looked at his phone and muttered so low that I couldn't tell if he was making words or just sounds.

Finally, he put down the device, gently rested the palm of his hand on the table, and told me, "I'll let you know closer to the weekend."

We exchanged numbers and agreed to keep in touch. The rain had slowed a little and we left the gas station. After hugging each other as if we had known each other all our lives, we went our separate ways.

The Thrush messaged me two days later. He had gotten some. Although he had never personally tried this variety before, they'd come highly recommended. Who had recommended them, I had no clue. I pictured a bunch of Thrush clones in a conference room on the top floor of a skyscraper exchanging acid reviews. He told me it was called Cartoon Network and that the tabs cost a hundred and fifty pesos each. I asked him for three, just in case, because LSD was hard to come by. He said he was going to be in my neighborhood later in the week and that he could bring them to me. I gave him my address.

That night, I met Romina for dinner. We went to a pizza place near her house. Romina arrived late, like always. As soon as she sat down at the table, she told me how much she hated her new boss. I listened to her rant, amused that what bothered her about her new boss was the same as what had annoyed her about the previous one. But everything work-related annoyed Romina. We had each already eaten three slices when I told her I had gotten acid. This news excited her. We discussed organizing something chill, either at her house or mine, with just a few people from our inner circle to ensure that we could enjoy a good trip. Romina loved the idea, but she wasn't going to be able to make it until the weekend after next. She was planning to go to the Mar del Plata Film Festival with some friends, Naty and Sol, who I didn't know. She asked me if I wanted to join them. I didn't have any plans, so I said yes. The idea was to go in Naty's car and rent an apartment there from Friday afternoon to Tuesday morning.

Although Romina was the least organized person I had ever met, she always assumed the role of coordinator in any group activity she got involved in: trips, events, parties. The planning always ended up being haphazard and chaotic. The next morning, I received an email from her, CC'd to Naty and Sol. The email included a list of links to available apartments with non-correlated numbering. Each also had a brief description and comments from Romina with the responses, or lack thereof, from the owners she had contacted. Next, there was another list—this one with consecutive numbering—of her five favorites. Finally, Romina asked us to each list our own five favorites. I clicked each link but ended up confused. Most of the listings in Romina's favorites were not in the first list and those that were didn't have any clarifications. Everything became even more chaotic when Naty and Sol replied. They listed different favorites than what Romina had chosen, though the two of them mostly seemed to share the same opinions. They insisted on booking a place with a separate room for themselves, and it had to offer linen and towels because bringing their own would take up too much space in their bags. All afternoon, emails stating preferences and tastes came and went every five minutes. I didn't feel like being part of the back-and-forth, so I just said I was fine with whatever they decided, but everyone wanted something different—amenities, views, and locations—which ultimately meant different apartments. They couldn't agree. In one of the last emails of the day, Romina was clearly furious because no one had made a decision, yet she refused to arbitrate or choose from the various options floating around, even though she was in charge of planning. As the days went by, I began to doubt whether or not the trip was going to happen. With no decision made and only a few days left, Romina set a deadline: by the end of the night we had to decide from a new, updated list of available apartments. Of the five listed, the same as before but now with different numbering, Naty and Sol chose two different options. I remained silent. Sometimes I was afraid of Romina. The matter was abruptly resolved the next day when Romina reserved a new apartment that hadn't appeared in any previous list or email. "Sounds good," we all answered.

The Thrush stopped by my place the night before the trip. I got in the elevator to go downstairs and open the front door of the building. I had the money in my hand, as if I were receiving a pizza delivery. I could see him behind the glass of the front door, leaning against the side wall, dressed in his black running tights, black t-shirt, and cap. He clutched a bottle of blue Gatorade and his skin shined with sweat. I couldn't get my head around the fact that he was such a sporty guy. When he saw me, he waved and smiled. I opened the door, and he greeted me with a friendly kiss on the cheek. The beads of fresh sweat that ran down his face pressed into my cheeks and stuck to me. I held the door open, intending to do our business right there, but he simply walked in. I tried to think of a polite excuse not to let him in, but I couldn't come up with anything, and suddenly we were in the elevator and, soon enough, on my floor.

Once in my flat, he went out to the balcony and took a deep breath, puffing out his chest and saying, "Such nice fresh air you have flowing here" even though he'd come from the same street that the balcony overlooked. Then he walked around the apartment, exploring, giving himself a tour. I stood next to the dining room table and watched him enter and leave each room in turn. In an attempt to expedite the transaction, I told him that I'd had a long day, but it had the opposite effect.

"Mine was pretty shitty too. I fought with my boss. Should we smoke one to relax?"

Before I could answer, he dropped onto the couch and began to roll a joint. I stood there looking at him, unsure if I felt annoyed or pleased. I didn't know whether I wanted to smoke. Once the joint was ready, he stood up and noticed that he had left a sweat mark on the sofa's leather upholstery. He apologized and tried to clean it with his t-shirt, which only spread it more, like a layer of shiny wax. I told him not to worry, although it did make me a little bit sick to see that bright halo where I usually sat to have dinner.

"This sofa is nice, huh?" the Thrush said while he softly caressed the cushions and backrest. "Kind of a Menemist[1] retro style."

"Yeah, it was left in a warehouse. It used to be in the office of a friend's father. She let me have it when she found out I was looking for one," I answered, proud of having rescued it and given it new life.

"This couch was in an office? Of *course*. Crazy parties must have happened right here. Can you imagine all the girls that must have sat their naked butts on these cushions?" he said, excited, with his eyes wide. After staring at the sofa for a moment, he got serious. "You should reupholster it. Or don't sit on it naked unless you want to get pregnant."

I burst out laughing, and I couldn't stop. The Thrush started listing all the characters, public figures, and stars who might have partied on my couch. By the time he'd made it to Yuyito González[2], my phone dinged. It was a message from Sol to a group chat entitled MARDEL that she had created. She wanted to let the rest of us know that two more

---

1. Carlos Saul Menem was twice president of Argentina in the 90s. During his administration, he implemented economic policies such as massive privatizations and a monetary regime of convertibility with the dollar, which was socially and economically devastating for the country. However, it did allow certain classes to access to a first-world way of life. Those times are often referred as "pizza with champagne" Since there were many scandals around him—parties and showgirls, etc.—saying something is very menemist is a reference to partying and that kind of lavish lifestyle
2. Stage name of an Argentine *vedette* (showgirl) who was very successful in the 1980s and linked to many affairs and sex scandals with politicians and businessmen.

people, friends of hers, would be joining us on our trip to Mar del Plata. They could sleep in the extra beds in the living room, if nobody had a problem with it. She argued that this way we would be able to divide costs between more people. I did have a problem with it. My laughter vanished in a second. My face turned as cold and serious as a tombstone. Four people sleeping in the living room of a small apartment seemed like too many. I began talking out loud to myself while the Thrush stared at me, trying to be understanding and supportive, saying "of course" or "whatever" after each uttered complaint or claim.

"What are we going to save, fifty pesos? Fifty pesos is, like, a pack of smokes. Why don't they sleep in her and Naty's room, since they insisted so much on having their own separate space," I said, indignant, smoking one cigarette after another without looking away from my phone screen in case someone answered.

The Thrush tried to distract me by telling me an absurd story about a friend of his, but I couldn't focus on anything he was saying. The thought of waking up in the morning and having to step over someone on my way to the toilet was stressing me out. We might as well have booked bunks in a hostel dormitory.

Even though the Thrush advised me to wait for someone else to answer first, I fired off a message, unable to refrain: "I think maybe four sleeping in the living room is too much, right?" No one answered. The chat was still silent when the Thrush left after midnight.

At the door, he told me, "If they drive you too crazy, just drop a tab in the *mate*[3] water and laugh your ass off."

The next morning, I woke to a message from Romina saying there were six beds in the living room and that it wouldn't be any problem for the extra friends to join us and

---

3. Traditional Argentine infusion that consists of placing a mix of herbs called *yerba* in a small container, which is called a *mate*, to which hot water is added over and over again and sucked with a special straw until it loses flavor. It is commonly shared.

sleep there. I felt instantly guilty. She changed the subject, thank God, to say she was bringing a hair straightener and asked if anyone had a hair dryer. Even though I don't use one, I said I was taking mine. I wanted to show that I did have the capacity to share, after all. I also announced that I was bringing mate, a thermos, yerba, shampoo, mouthwash, toothpaste, and toilet paper for everyone, including the two new additions, and that I was going to buy some snacks for the trip as well. No one answered. The chat remained silent until the afternoon when Naty sent a message saying the extra toilet paper wasn't necessary because Sol's friends weren't coming with us after all. Seconds later, Sol also chimed in. She wasn't going to take any snacks ("the industrial type," she clarified) for the trip, but she'd baked an organic seedless tangerine cake. I felt a little slighted, but I replied "Awesome!!! So excited about the cake!!!" even though I've never really been into sweet stuff. I'm more the salty type. I refrained from saying anything about the friends who weren't coming. I didn't mention the acid either, preferring to have it be a surprise.

We planned to leave from Naty's house on Friday afternoon. I got there earlier than the time we'd agreed on, but I rang the bell anyway. Naty answered through the intercom and I introduced myself as Romina's friend.

"Already? It's early," she said and hung up.

For a second, I thought she was going to keep me outside waiting, but as soon as I took out a cigarette I heard the sound of the front door being unlocked. When she opened the door to her flat, her face looked strangely familiar. She was skinny, not very tall, with round, bulging, light-blue eyes and medium-short blonde hair with her bangs combed to one side. Except for her hairstyle, she looked very similar to Sofía, a friend who had just moved to China to be the onsite manager of the Chinese supply line of the company where she worked, and Karina, a girl who'd worked in the purchase department at my previous job.

"Do you want a glass of water?" Naty asked.

"Yes, I'd love one," I told her, trying to be polite. I wasn't actually thirsty.

When Naty brought it to me, I couldn't keep myself from staring at her, not only trying to figure whether she looked more like Sofía or Karina, but surprised because I had just realized that Sofía and Karina looked so much like each other and they both worked in the same area: purchasing.

"Do you work in purchasing?" I asked.

"Huh?" She looked confused. "No, no, nothing like that, not at all. God. I work in film and advertising."

From the tone of her voice, it seemed she despised the profession of my friends who looked like her. Or she despised me. While we waited for Romina and Sol, Naty didn't say a word. Total silence. She appeared and disappeared down a hallway, bringing identical green plastic bags, stuffed with things, that she kept putting in her backpack. I wanted to break the silence, but I couldn't think of anything to say. Maybe she was annoyed that I'd arrived early and now she couldn't get ready alone in peace. It would have bothered me. I sat down in a chair at the round dining room table and sipped the water. I wanted to smoke but I was certain it wasn't allowed. Her house was perfectly organized. It seemed static, motionless, like the set of a play. An ornament that hung from the ceiling above a mustard-colored sofa was the only thing that broke this illusion. Its thin wires held up several colored glass circles that spun softly, seeming to float in the air. I envied her a little. Everything seemed meticulously considered and selected, especially compared to my house, which had been decorated with donations or things I'd found on the street, in warehouses, or in the back room of my grandmother's house.

"Your place is super nice," I told her next time she appeared in the hallway.

"Yes, I know," she answered without humility. "You said you were bringing a hair dryer, right? So, did you? If you did, I won't bring mine."

"Yeah I have one," I answered quickly, feeling as proud as if I had passed an extremely difficult test.

"Well, the girls are a block away, so let's go down. We have to pick up the car from the car wash place around the corner," she said.

I barely had time to put down the glass, stand up, and grab my things before she was in the elevator.

Sol and Romina were standing in the street. Sol was very tiny, skinny, wearing intense red lipstick. Her hair was short and blonde, and her bangs were styled the same way as Naty's.

"Hi! I'm Carolina. How are you?" I greeted her.

"Hi!" she answered with a big smile. "How are you? I'm Sol." She had a high-pitched voice. She gave me a noisy kiss and set to fixing her bangs with her small hands.

I didn't get to say hi to Romina because Naty was already at the corner, hurrying us toward the car wash. Except for me, everyone had brought a backpack. I had a small pink carry-on suitcase.

Naty was walking super fast. Sol kept pace right behind her, moving her tiny legs quickly. The wheels of my carry-on kept getting stuck in the cracks in the sidewalk, which caused me to walk clumsily, more slowly than the others. Romina moved at a much more relaxed pace, waiting for me to catch up so she could tell me about work and her stupid boss. She was outraged that she hadn't been allowed to leave the office early, but she knew she couldn't complain too much since she had taken the following Monday off. To ensure she had a three-day weekend, she had used the one "feminine day" her company gave to women every month for when they had their period. She'd told her boss she had some gynecological tests scheduled, but she suspected they knew she was lying because today, not only she had taken her backpack to the office, but when she was leaving for her lunch break her boss's assistant had recommended some talks that were going to take place as part of the Film Festival. I wanted to say something about the whole thing, but I felt so stupid dragging my suitcase down the street trying to keep up I remained silent.

"Are you bringing a lot of shit?" Romina shouted to me while she stood on the corner, waiting for me to catch up so we could cross the street.

I felt even more stupid. I mentally reviewed everything I was carrying. Maybe I had gone a little overboard. I'd always hated people who carried a lot of luggage. I thought they were idiots. Now, I was the idiot. That made me feel mad, and I took it out on Romina. I felt like she also thought I was an idiot.

"Romina, you're constantly complaining about your work," I told her when I caught up with her, looking at her with a bored expression. "Why don't you just quit?"

"I'm not complaining about my job, I'm just telling you I think they realized what I was up to," she reproached me. "And I am not quitting. Ever. If they want to get rid of me, they'll have to fire me and pay me severance and everything."

I didn't respond. She was kind of right, but, at the same time, she kind of wasn't. She remained lost in thought while we waited to cross at the stoplight. Naty and Sol, without even looking back, were already turning the next corner.

"Well, I bought a 100 SPF sunscreen, just in case, so I don't come back with a tan."

I told her that even if she stayed in Buenos Aires over the weekend, she could get a tan by sitting on a rooftop or a balcony or riding a bike or just walking down the street.

"Yeah, but I'm not the kind of person who likes sunbathing anyway. Besides, I hate sports. You know that," she answered, irritated by my hypothesis. She started walking faster, leaving me behind.

When we arrived at the car wash, Naty was in the

middle of a shouting match with a short, fat guy. Around them, shiny cars emerged one after the other. Sol briefed us on the situation: the car wash guys didn't remember where they had left Naty's car. Once she calmed down, they asked her to identify her keys from a big bowl full of keys. Then, with those keys in the fat guy's hands, we followed him, in a single line, to a car that had been parked half a block from the car wash. He assured us it was Naty's. Naty assured him it was not. He was fully convinced that it was indeed hers, and when he put the key in the door and was able to unlock it with Naty's keys, he placed his hand on his chest Maradona[4] style and exclaimed, "Hop in, I'll drive you ladies anywhere you want to go." We all laughed, except for Naty. The fat guy squeezed himself into the car, smiling, but when he tried to turn the key in the ignition, he couldn't.

"I told you this wasn't my car. I've had this experience before, you know, confusedly opening other cars that look like mine, but when you try to start them, you can't. The keys unlock every car of this same model," Naty told him with an icy tone. She took the keys out of his hands.

The fat guy got out of the car. He looked disappointed and kept his head down after his scolding. We all walked back to the car wash. I continued pulling my suitcase behind me, feeling increasingly stupid. At the car wash, one of the employees, who was wearing knee-high rain boots, an unofficial Boca Juniors t-shirt, and torn and sagging jeans that left half of his underwear hanging out, pointed us toward a different corner where Naty's car actually was.

The four of us stood behind the car. Naty huffed and opened the trunk. She took out a poster that a friend of hers had left there after finding it on the street after a party. It

---

4. Diego Armando Maradona was an Argentine futbol player, considered to this day to be one of the best of all time, despite his controversial lifestyle. He often walked with his shoulders back, puffing out his chest.

showed a group of holographic cats and dogs. Without so much as glancing at the poster, she extended it to Sol and ordered her to throw it away. But Sol held it in her tiny hands and began to move it slowly from side to side, laughing while the dogs turned into cats and the cats turned into dogs, surrounded by psychedelic colors and shapes that appeared and disappeared. Romina and I found it hilarious and we couldn't stop laughing until Naty yelled at us.

"Hey! Let's start loading up the luggage. Yours first, since it's the biggest," she said, pointing at me.

She seemed to know how stupid I felt, how much it bothered me to be the one who'd brought the most stuff. Or maybe she was just envious. My luggage was prettier than hers. It was a new, pink, micro-perforated carry-on with a semi-hard shell, and hers was just a black-and-khaki backpack with old, worn-out wheels.

After loading the luggage, we got in the car. Sol sat up front, while Romina and I were in back. We immediately had to open all the windows. The car wash had gone overboard with the air freshener. Three tablets hung from the rearview mirror. It was too much. There was a strong, bitter, spicy smell, so intense we couldn't breathe. We weren't able to put our finger on what scent it was, exactly. In an attempt at identification, Romina began to list essences, searching the web on her phone. Sol and I agreed that it could be myrrh. Naty didn't care that myrrh was considered a sacred plant, offering universal protection against the evil eye, spells and witchcraft. She ripped the three tablets from the rearview mirror and threw them out the window. The smell dissipated as we got on the highway. Naty told us to pay attention, that at some point we would have to take the cutoff to route 2.

"The GPS will let you know," I told her.

"I can't drive and look at the GPS at the same time. You look at it and let me know," Naty answered.

Until we reached the exit, the atmosphere inside the car was tense. Nobody could relax or start a conversation without being interrupted by Naty asking if we were paying attention, if the exit was coming up, if we were looking at the map and the route signs. Before any of us could see any indication of the cutoff, a voice from Naty's GPS said, "in 500 meters, keep right and take the detour to Route 2"

Nobody said anything until Naty took the exit. As soon as we were on it, Naty started talking about her previous night. She spoke in a tone that was sweet, tender, and almost stupid. She told us how she had been working late on the set of a shoot for an advertisement campaign, putting particular emphasis on the director of the commercial who she was "soooooooo in love with" because he was "a genius" and "super mega ultra hot." Romina and Sol asked a lot of questions about him and about her night, but I kept quiet. I was also silent as Sol began telling us how exhausting it was for her to manage the construction work on the house that she had just bought with her boyfriend, which she was renovating, and how awful it had been that the natural gas had been shut off for two weeks because of a poorly installed connection in the heaters had almost caused her house to explode. I didn't know them well enough to make any comments, reflections, or suggestions about the problems and events in their lives, but I was interested in listening to them. I didn't have a boyfriend, nor was I even interested in anyone. I imagined scenes from their stories while I looked out the window, pretending to be completely indifferent. When we were passing through Chascomús, Naty addressed me and began a comprehensive interrogation. First, she wanted to know where Romina and I had met, then how old I was, if I lived alone or with a partner, what I had studied at university, what I did for a living, and so on, a ping pong match of questions and answers. I intentionally gave monosyllabic responses, unburdened by any sort of explanation. I enjoyed leaving her wanting additional information she would not receive. It was a way to be at once boring and mysterious. Sol would exclaim "Oh, how cool" or "Oh, awesome" to everything I said, but Naty was never satisfied. She continued her investigation and Romina often embellished my answers with her own commentary in order to to develop them or make them more specific. At one point Naty got tired, or gave up, and went straight to the topic of the festival and the films we had chosen. Naty and Sol were surprised that we had already gotten all our tickets. Romina had gotten nine and I had gotten six. They only had gotten two each.

"Oh God! Are you really going to watch all that? I'm only interested in seeing the ones that are actually in the competition, not the panorama ones. You know they just show whatever there, don't you? You definitely chose from those, right?" Naty said, with a little smirk and touch of sarcasm.

"Yes, Naty, they probably picked all of those," Sol answered. "We don't watch those," she told us, turning around and shaking her head.

"Let's see, tell me, which ones did you choose?" Naty asked, looking at the back seat in the rearview mirror.

I said nothing. I had no idea what panorama or competition meant. I thought they were all in competition at a festival. Luckily, it seemed like Romina knew how the whole thing worked. She said that some were indeed from panorama, but not all of them, and she listed the titles, which she had written down in a list on her phone. There was only one film in common between our list and Sol and Naty's list, about a broke Ukrainian boxer, but we had reserved tickets for different showtimes.

"Awww, look how cute the movies that you chose are!" Naty said, with an obviously ironic and haughty tone, laughing.

"I find them all very appealing" I replied, serious, although I had agreed to whatever Romina had suggested because I hadn't felt like doing much research.

"Me too. And that's the purpose of going to a film festival, you know, to watch a lot of movies," Romina added, a bit irritated.

"That's right. The first one we have scheduled is today at twelve, right after we arrive," I said, supporting Romina.

"Today? At midnight?" Naty asked, surprised.

"You're going to arrive and go straight to a cinema?" Sol asked.

"Exactly. It seems to be an excellent film, and if we hadn't picked this showtime, it would have conflicted with the others that we want to see," Romina explained with pride.

I actually agreed with Sol and Naty: it was insane to go to the movies after riding in a car for five hours, but I just nodded my head, perfectly playing my cinephile role. I could have been a double agent in another life. Or an actress.

"The thing I'm just dying to do is go to the opening party. It's super VIP, but I know people who know people who know other people that can definitely put me on the list," Naty boasted.

"Ah! That's amazing! We can all meet after our movie and go together!" Romina exclaimed, excited.

Honestly, I was also excited. I actually would have rather gone straight to the party and skipped the movie all together. I thought I could persuade Romina to do the same, but Naty crushed my hopes, saying, "Mmm. Yeah. Well, we'll have to see if we can all get in."

I would have loved to say, "Well, we'll have to see if I brought enough acid for all of us," but I kept it to myself, pursing my lips.

For the rest of the trip, there were two conversations, one in the front of the car, and one in the back. Sol and Naty. Romina and me. We talked excitedly about the last trip Romina had gone on, backpacking around Peru. In the background, we could hear Naty talking unendingly about the director she was "super into." Her voice grew louder and louder, then suddenly she asked us to quiet down. She said we were making a lot of noise. I automatically apologized. The volume of my voice does tend to rise to unexpected levels.

"It's just that your voices are overlapping each other in a chaotic jumble and I can't hear what Sol is saying." I looked at Sol. She was putting on concealer, touching up her red lipstick, and combing her bangs in the visor mirror.

It was almost night when Sol took the organic seedless tangerine cake out of a tupperware and offered it to us. Naty refused.

"First I need to have a *mate*," she said.

I saw her eyes fix on mine in the rearview mirror. I found the yerba and prepared the *mate*. Although Naty kept repeating her need for an urgent mate, I respected tradition by starting the round with Romina. Then it went to Sol and, finally, to Naty. Each time I served Naty, I filled the *mate* to the brim, and she kept spilling, saying "*ay ay ay*" as the hot water fell into her lap. I kept pouring and passing the *mate* around until everyone else had had enough. I drank the last of it myself. Everyone praised the tangerine cake. To me, it tasted just okay, but I still asked Sol for the recipe. "Pleeeease, you have to share it with me!"

After five hours, we arrived at Mar del Plata. Naty needed detailed guidance as we entered the city. Despite our repeated instruction, Naty kept missing the street where we had to turn. She insisted she wasn't allowed to turn there, even though both the street signs and the GPS indicated that she could, so we inevitably circled around several times. Romina texted Sebastián, the owner of the apartment we had rented, so that he could direct us.

"He is not answering," Romina said.

"Call him, Romina," Naty commanded, gripping the steering wheel as if we were in a life-or-death situation.

"Oof. I don't feel like talking on the phone," Romina huffed.

"You call him, Sol," Naty commanded again, her knuckles turning white.

"Me? I don't have any credit left," Sol said, softly.

"Here, use my phone," Romina told her as she handed over her phone. "He has my number."

Sol called. On her second attempt, Sebastián picked up. Sol greeted him as if she were Romina, since that's whose phone she was calling from. Trying to explain that Romina didn't feel like talking and that she was someone else was too long and unnecessary. She put him on speaker, and despite the extremely precise directions he provided, we went around in circles two or three more times, until, somehow, miraculously, we arrived.

Sebastián was waiting for us inside a white car in front of the building. He got out as we parked and started unloading our things.

"Romina and friends, right?" He asked. "I watched you go by a few times," he said. He came towards us laughing, but not in an *I'm-laughing-about-how-stupid-you-girls-are* kind of way. Or maybe just a little, but it was mostly in a *so-cool-you-made-it* way. He was around thirty years old, a big rugby player type of guy, a little chubby, wearing jeans and a plaid shirt. One by one, he greeted us with a soft handshake and a kiss on the cheek, repeating his name each time. It was like a formal greeting ceremony that we had to engage in and which we performed in a very clumsy way while we took our suitcases and backpacks out of the car, bumping into each other. He instantly recognized Sol's unmistakable voice from having spoken to her on the phone and kept calling her Romina. None of us bothered to explain that she wasn't Romina; that she was Sol and Romina was Romina, leaving him mixed up about the names. He showed us how to open the front gates. There was no actual key, but just a round piece of plastic, no bigger than a small coin, that had a sensor inside. When you placed it in a specific area, the gates unlocked. The lobby door was always open. The door to the apartment did have a key, a small and old one, like something that might open a teenager's diary from the 80s. There were two keyrings, each with a sensor and a key. One had a pink plastic tag and the other had a purple plastic tag. As soon as Sebastian held them out, Sol grabbed the purple one and put it in her pocket. Romina took the pink.

The building was very old. The hallways were freezing. They looked like the ones from the hotel in *The Shining*. The apartment doors were antique, cream colored with aqua-green-to-pastel-light-blue moldings and brass handles carved with arabesques. Once inside, it was apparent the apartment had been renovated, though in a peculiar, selective way. The floors in the living room, kitchen, and bathroom were laid with shiny-white new tiles, but the original dark hardwood floor had been left in the bedroom. I wondered if there hadn't been enough money to finish the renovation or if they had miscalculated the amount of tile they had needed to order. In the living room, there was a table made of glass and upholstered in cheap synthetic red leather. There were also some black metal chairs, two small beds with extra mattresses under each one, and a TV with DIRECTV. Sebastián showed us how to turn it on by pressing a complicated combination of buttons on three different remotes. He surfed through the channels until he came to a show hosted by a man who looked like a doll: orange-tanned with bleached hair and a gold earring in his right ear. The panelists on the show discussed entertainment, gossip, and current political issues. Everyone on the show shouted over everybody else. For a few minutes, Sebastian remained hypnotized, his eyes fixed on the screen. I continued looking around. I went into the kitchen, where there was a refrigerator from the 1970s—which turned off and on loudly—a yellowish microwave, and a classic, non-electric, metal kettle. The kitchen cabinets were probably original, brown formica with worn metal handles. The bathroom, which was small but had a bathtub (and a bidet) had been completely renovated and now had a single row of glass blocks in the middle of the wall, stretching from end to end. Half of them seemed to look into the living room, while the other half looked into the kitchen. I got the impression you might be able to monitor everything that was happening on the other side, but when I tried to spy on everyone, I couldn't distinguish anything. I left the bathroom feeling a little disappointed and confused.

I walked around looking for the balcony, but I couldn't find it because it didn't exist. In fact, not only was there no balcony, the apartment only had one window. It was at the back of the only real room. The wall between the bedroom and the living room was fake, a giant MDF panel with a rectangular opening in the middle, a kind of horizontal window that stretched from side to side, making it feel like a hospital nursery. On the right side of the fake wall, there was a glass door with an orange curtain behind it that connected the living room and the bedroom. I entered the room and approached the singular window to admire the view. The beach was right across the street. I could hear the surf, and, even in the darkness, I saw the white foam of breaking waves. To one side was the pier, with the fishermen's club at the end of it, its aura a deep, relaxed French blue. The glow of its soft illumination distinguished it from the tired yellow-orange of the lights on the street and promenade. On the other end of the beach was the casino, flashing spastically in meaningless multicolor. No one was on the street, and the nighttime landscape, with the sound of the ocean and the lightshow, was beautiful. I could have looked at it for hours if it weren't for the fact that being in that hospital nursery bedroom gave me the creeps. The bedspread covering the double bed, which Naty and Sol were going to share, was an antique, white satin matelassé quilt with ruffles. On each of the ancient bedside tables sat a ceramic lamp with a yellowish lampshade. Set on top of the one on the right was a plaster figure of a woman holding a basket of flowers on her head. Her eyes lacked pupils, which gave the impression that the woman was watching you, no matter where you stood in the room. A large water stain in the corner of the ceiling ran down the wall like varicose veins before disappearing behind the headboard, making it look like the room was melting. It might have been the bedroom of a recently deceased great-grandmother who had been forgotten by her family. I left, swearing to stick to the modern side of the apartment from now on.

Sebastián told us that there were extra blankets in the closet and that the gas heater was already turned on. Sol asked him where the flue for the heater was, and he explained that it was an internal system. Sol pressed the issue. It was obvious she had been traumatized by the faulty connections that had nearly burned down her new house, almost killing her and her boyfriend. Even though Sebastian insisted that everything was perfectly safe, his explanations left Sol unsatisfied. She repeated the same question over and over again, until Sebastián stopped answering her.

Romina took out cash to pay him for the days we were staying and asked where we could go for quick, easy dinner, since the movie we were seeing started in an hour. He told us about an Irish pub in the area and gave us directions. He spoke quickly, and his eyes shone with excitement. He looked like someone talking about his kid's first steps—or first whatever—describing the event to someone who didn't have, didn't want, and couldn't stand children. Then, he asked about the festival. Did we already know what films we were going to see? Could we recommend some to him? His questions were directed to the whole group, but his eyes stayed fixed on Sol.

When I'd started to think that he might just decide to stay with us for the whole weekend, Naty stood in front of him and said, "I'll go down to open the front gate for you."

He gave each of us a little goodbye kiss. No handshake this time. Before he left, he pointed at his phone and told Sol that, if she felt like it, she should call or send him a message.

Romina and I were short on time, and we were hungry. We threw our things on the living room beds, ready to grab something to eat before the movie. It wouldn't get out until late, when everything might be closed. We used our phones to find a map to the theater. It was only five blocks away, and Romina noticed that there was a bar across the street from it. There were some food options and it had a rating of 4.5 stars. Sol and Naty, on the other hand, began to unpack and slowly arrange their things in the nursery. They tried on different outfits in front of the mirror and went in and out of the bathroom, first to pee, then to put on makeup and afterwards to fix their hair, disregarding the hurry we were in. I wanted to leave, but Romina said we should wait for them. Waiting inside the apartment, watching how slowly they were moving, started making me anxious. I was also desperate for a smoke, so I told Romina I would meet her downstairs.

Outside, the icy fresh air burned my nostrils. A few meters away from the building entrance, on the same block, there was a convenience store. I went to get a pack of cigarettes. More waiting. There was a long line of people waiting to recharge their bus passes. When it was finally my turn, the girl at the window told me that for anything other than recharging my bus pass, I should go directly inside the shop.

"Next in line," she said.

A little annoyed by having waited pointlessly, I entered through the side door, but there was no one else working there. Just the girl at the window. I stared at the empty counter. Some bananas hung from the ceiling. As I was about to say something to the window girl, another employee emerged from a door in the back, which I hadn't noticed because it was hidden between two shelves filled with crackers, cookies, and snacks. She was short and a bit plump, with long black hair tied in a seemingly endless braid. She was dressed in a completely different style than her coworker, who wore tight light-blue jeans and a short black top printed with the number 8. It was low-cut, and every other customer she dealt with stupidly commented on her tits. The second employee, on the other hand, wore a long colorful skirt, a turquoise long-sleeved T-shirt with a violet short-sleeved shirt over it. Her clothes were as faded as the homemade, knockoff Cheetos and potato chips in their thin, wrinkled plastic bags. I asked her for gum and a pack of cigarettes. She gave them to me. I paid in cash, apologizing for not having exact change. She got change from the register, which was at the other end of the counter, closer to the window. I stretched out my hand to receive it. As she gave me the money, she cradled my hand in hers and looked into my eyes.

In a tone that was soft and soothing, yet firm, she said, "May your clothes and shoes wear out, but may you live long and grow old."

For a millisecond I froze, feeling a bit lost and trying to comprehend, to decode the unexpected message, and she continued to stare at me. Her gaze was at once powerful and sweet. It made me nervous. My mind went blank.

I grinned shyly and said, "Thank you!"

I left quickly. At first I thought it was kind of cool. I couldn't help but smile as I walked back towards the building entrance. It felt kind of like if a guy I liked had just flirted with me. But I kept thinking about what she had said, the line replaying in my mind in an endless loop, and I realized that it wasn't so cool after all. I didn't want my clothes—much less my shoes, which had cost me an arm and a leg—to wear out. That would be an awful tragedy. I also didn't like the idea of getting old and wrinkled.

I sat on the front steps of the apartment building, smoking, picturing what I would be like as an old lady. It was hard. I saw myself exactly as I was, only with gray hair. My old lady self was riding dirt bikes, climbing mountains, partying on boats, and smoking long cigarettes next to a pool on a terrace overlooking the ocean. She had different outfits, but always wore the same pair of shoes. Three cigarettes and forty minutes later, when I had convinced myself it was time to start using anti-age serums, Romina, Naty, and Sol came out. We stood with the cold ocean wind blowing against our faces, silently looking at each other. Naty and Sol obviously didn't want to get something to eat with us, but neither said a word. I started to get anxious again, but my mouth was already dry from having smoked so much, and, no longer able to tolerate the staring contest, I suggested that, maybe, if they were okay with it, they could go one way and we could go another. Naty and Sol agreed immediately and offered to drive us to where we were going. Although I would have rather walked—I had already spent five hours in the car with them—once again I ended up in the back seat with Romina, giving Naty directions. Not only did I have to guide her to the cinema, but then I had to give her clear, very specific instructions on how to get where she wanted to go, as if she couldn't look it up on her GPS. I showed her the map on my phone, but shook her head and she told me she didn't even understand where she was. So I explained how many blocks straight ahead she had to go, how many to the left, and how many to the right. When she finally understood, Romina and I got out, crossed the plaza, and entered the bar.

There was a band playing inside. The only free table was right next to the stage, and, having no other choice, we took it. I couldn't decide if the music was good or not because the volume was at full blast, distorting the sounds and voices. Our menus were brought quickly. After checking the few food options they had, we decided on two *lomitos completos*[5] and a beer. The bar audience was assorted. There were some young couples, several groups of people over fifty, and a group of friends spread across several tables who all looked the same: they all wore caps with high and wide fronts and disproportionately large bills that covered their faces.

To save time, Romina went across the street to the cinema to print the tickets while I placed our order. When she came back, I was already having my first glass of beer. I thought that's why she looked disappointed, but it wasn't.

---

5. A popular kind of sandwich, featuring a medium-thick slice of beef, melted cheese, a slice of ham, lettuce, tomato, and onion.

She told me that she had made a mistake. The movie didn't start at 12. It had started at 11:30. Since we had missed it, we relaxed and started eating and drinking without any rush. We decided we could see the other option, one that started at 1:10. I took advantage of the fact that we were alone and told Romina I had brought three tabs of acid.

"Three?" Romina asked, her eyes wide.

"Yeah, just in case," I said, laughing.

"I'm not going to take more than a quarter." she told me. She sounded a little scared.

"Well, just take a bit and see how it hits you."

"Yeah, I don't know whether Naty or Sol will want any." She looked thoughtful.

I wasn't altogether sure I even wanted to take acid with them, so to change the subject I asked her how much time we had left until the other movie started. We still had time. We poured out the last of the pitcher and ordered another one, then another, then one more, and when we looked at the time again, we found we had missed that movie too.

When the band finished their set, people started leaving, and in no time there was nobody left in the bar except for us and some women drinking tea in the back. Romina sent several messages to Naty to see what they were up to, telling them to join us, or that we would meet up with them, but Naty neither read them nor responded. We were already feeling a little bit drunk and didn't want to go to sleep. We walked to another bar that Romina found online and drank more beers. The place was pretty crowded, and, according to our calculations, seven out of ten guys were wearing caps, the same kind with big visors and wide fronts. Romina and I agreed that there weren't that many cap wearers in Buenos Aires. At dawn, we were the only ones left and we were politely kicked out. Romina refused to walk back to the apartment because she was afraid it might be dangerous, so we took a taxi that miraculously appeared on the deserted street at the exact moment we exited the bar.

As we got in the taxi, the driver greeted us with "Good morning." We found that ridiculous: it was only 4:30.

"You can only make that joke after six, sir" Romina said.

Worried that he would get mad and kick us out of the cab, I tried not to laugh, but I did anyway. I told him where we were going. He took off at full speed, tires screeching, accelerating faster and faster through the empty streets, taking the corners sharply, not stopping at any lights. A small red bag hung from the rearview mirror and swayed with the movement of the car. Sitting in the back seat, so did we. The bag looked like an air freshener, but the car smelled musty. I asked what was in the bag, and he told me that its contents were private. Romina began to make absurd speculations about what it could be, out loud, just to irritate him. I looked out the window, again trying to contain my laughter. The driver remained silent, speeding up even more. Around half an hour later, we were still in the taxi and we realized that he had gone way too far. After again telling him our destination, he got lost several more times, so we pulled out our phone maps to guide him. He was visibly reluctant to follow our directions. He got angry, claiming we hadn't given him the right address in the first place. But we assured him we had, and, after all, he was from Mar Del Plata and we weren't. He was a taxi driver and we weren't. So he should have known how to get to our rental without issue. He left us at the corner of our block, insisting that he couldn't pull up to the door. We didn't feel like arguing anymore so we got out, and as soon as we were both out of the car, he muttered something we couldn't make out and Romina slammed the taxi door really hard. He took off, tires screeching again, and we walked towards the main door of the apartment building in a clumsy zigzag, laughing our asses off.

It took Romina a while to find the not-key, the round plastic sensor thing. While we were still laughing about our taxi driver, she held it up to the designated area, as Sebastian had instructed us. The lock clanked and a light turned green, but the gate wouldn't open, even if we pushed it. We tried several more times with no luck. We just couldn't open it. We looked it over from top to bottom searching for some trick, some lever or button we might have missed but found nothing. We tried to see if any of the other keys would work, but there was no keyhole to put them in. I reached through the bars and tried to push the gate open from the inside, but that didn't work either. Were we at the wrong building? The "Monte Carlo" sign out front told us that it was, without a doubt, our building. We were about to call Naty and Sol for help, when we tried once more. Defeated, I leaned against the fence at the same time Romina was holding the plastic sensor in the same place, and then, because of my weight on it, the bars that I thought were part of the fence swung open. We had been trying to open the gate by pushing on the fixed fence. We couldn't contain our laughter and when neither of us could properly insert the teenager diary key in the apartment lock we started shrieking with glee.

We burst into the apartment, tears in our eyes, and exploded into even more laughter when, through the window that looked into the bedroom, we saw Naty and Sol sitting on the bed like newborn babies waiting to be fed in a hospital nursery.

"Where were you?" Sol asked us from behind the glass.

"We missed the movie and we went to have some beers there...around...," Romina answered as she threw herself on her living room bed.

"And then we spent an hour trying to open the door because...," I started to tell them, laughing, but Naty interrupted me.

"Can you please keep your voice down? You're shouting." She gave us a look of hatred.

I sat on the bed. I felt like I had been scolded by my mom. Romina and I started whispering. After a while, Naty came out of the nursery, heading to the bathroom, but she stopped halfway.

"We went to the opening party in the white tent next to the casino and we saw Benjamín Vicuña.[6] He's amazing. And so, *so* hot," Naty told us without having been asked.

"I sent you several messages to see what you were up to," Romina told her.

"Oh yeah? Did you? That's a shame. I never got them," Naty said, playing it cool. She fixed her bangs and kept walking towards the bathroom. I fell asleep before she came out.

I woke up the next day by falling out of bed. The mattress was sagging on one side and I slid out. I climbed to the good side of the mattress and tried to find a comfortable position, but I sank back into the dip and my entire blanket fell to the floor. I got up and took out the extra mattress from under the bed and exchanged it with mine. While I was making the switch, surprised by how a single mattresses could be so heavy, Romina woke up with a sudden, spastic, almost Olympic jump, which left her sitting on the bed, her hair covering her face, saying indivual words that didn't form coherent sentences. Her tone was sleepy and worried. I somehow deciphered what she was trying to say: she thought I was going for a run, and, since she had a movie early that morning, she was afraid I would take the keys with me and leave her locked inside. I told her to chill, that I was just changing the mattress. I went back to bed, but I couldn't get back to sleep. I kept thinking about how I was going to be an old lady one day, and there wasn't anything I could do about it. I was unable to consciously grasp the actual idea of aging, yet I could already feel it happening. I was searching for wrinkles on my face with my fingers when Romina got up to take a shower. She had realized that she was already running late for the movie. I couldn't stand lying sleepless in bed, so I went to the kitchen to prepare some *mate*.

The apartment was totally dark except for the light coming through the glass-brick wall of the bathroom. While

6. A Chilean actor that works in many Argentinian soap operas and shows who is (supposedly) very hot.

heating the water in the non-electric kettle, I stared at the fruit Naty had brought and left on top of the microwave. Right in the middle of the appliance was a red apple with the sticker still on it. A huge, misshapen tangerine sat on the left edge. On top of them, arching between the two, was a banana that was about to go bad. I was hungry, and I really wanted to eat the apple, to take one bite and then another and another. Except I couldn't stop thinking about how Naty would react when she found out that her apple had disappeared. Or maybe nothing would happen, but I thought that was unlikely. She would say something, at least. Where was her apple? Who ate her apple? Or she might simply state that she wanted to eat an apple and there wasn't an apple to eat. I could hear her voice, her vicious, annoying, mean, haughty tone, echoing in my head. But I was so hungry. I took it and held it in both hands. It was beautiful. So red. So shiny. So perfectly shaped. Precious. Naty's apple suddenly seemed to be the last apple in the whole world. The idea of it made me even hungrier. I could hear my stomach growling. I was about to take a bite when I saw Naty's bulging eyes coming straight out of the apple, staring at me accusingly. The lines of the apple peel took the shape of her bangs. Her mouth appeared under the sticker, her lips red with lipstick, even redder than the apple itself, shouting, asking me if I had been the one who had eaten her exquisite apple, knowing well that I had been. Slowly, so as not to damage it in any way, I put the apple back on top of the microwave. I'd rather be hungry than have to listen to her inquisition about the missing apple, and, even worse, to have to answer politely because we weren't nearly close enough for me to tell her face to face that it was just a fucking apple and to fuck off.

Romina came out of the bathroom. She was almost ready to go, just missing her shoes. She had some *mate* with me in near total silence while putting on her boots. I went down with her, barefoot and in my pajamas, so I could open the front gate and keep the keys to go out later. The hallways were even colder than they had been the night before. The floor was icy. I felt thumbtacks of cold piercing the soles of my bare feet. They triggered chills that ran up my leg, across my core, and went all the way into my brain.

"Do you think that if I eat Naty's apple World War Three will break out?" I asked her, my teeth chattering, as we walked towards the staircase.

"I mean…" She hesitated for a moment, making a face. "I did blow dry my hair in the bathroom, just in case, because I knew she would complain about the noise."

Neither of us said anything else as we descended the stairs. Opening the door was like crossing a portal into another dimension. It was a spectacular day outside, full of people on the street and walking down the promenade by the beach. The apartment had been so dark that the sunlight hurt my eyes. It wasn't cold at all. On the contrary. It was hot, and the warm, humid air enveloped me like a heavy blanket. I walked with Romina to the convenience store to buy something to eat. I paid close attention to where I was walking, careful not to step on any glass, fresh chewing gum, or dog shit. The concrete was warm in the sun and it felt nice. Like the night before, there was a long line of people at the shop, and the same girl with big boobs was at the window. I told Romina to go straight inside, but we found the door closed.

"Hey! You two! Only through the window!" Big Boobs shouted from inside.

"I'm not going to charge my bus pass. We want to buy some stuff," I told her.

"It's all through the window!" she yelled at me again.

I was confused by the change in customer service. Being half-asleep didn't help. Luckily, the line was moving quickly. When it was our turn, I found the window girl's big boobs directly in my face. Again, she wore a low-cut shirt, maybe even more so than the one from the night before, but instead of the number eight, this one was printed with the words "fatal look" in large letters, which were a bit deformed due to how stretched the T-shirt was, far too small to adequately contain her big boobs. It was impossible not to look at her tits. They were magnetic. We asked for the five bananas that had been hanging from the ceiling since the night before, a big Cindor-brand chocolate milk that Romina wanted, and a Coke to help me get rid of the dryness in my mouth. I stood on the step in front of the window so I could peek inside. There was no sign of the other girl.

"Do you need anything else?" Big Boobs asked me, anxious to finish the transaction and move on to the next person in line. I wondered what her customer per minute ratio was, if she had a quota to hit.

"Nope, that's it." I handed her a hundred-peso bill. "Are you working alone today?"

"Yes," she answered, counting my change.

"And the other girl?" I asked her.

"She's not here" was the dry answer she gave while handing me my change and calling out to the next person in line. I was a bit disappointed.

Romina took a banana and her Cindor and headed to the cinema, her body moving as if she were running a marathon, but she was actually walking at an incredibly slow pace. I went back to the apartment with the other four bananas, drinking my Coke. Naty and Sol were still sleeping. I ate the largest banana of the four, staring at Naty's apple. Afterwards, I got dressed to go for a run, groping in the dark for my clothes and shoes, which were in my suitcase. I felt something behind me, and when I turned around, I saw Naty standing behind the nursery glass staring at me. I greeted her, but she ignored me. After a bit more staring, she left the nursery and went into the bathroom without saying a word. She was still in there when I left.

I ran along the path by the sea. It was so crowded that I had to pay close attention. I weaved through people, careful not to bump into anyone. It was a diverse crowd, made of a mix of locals from the Atlantic coast area, festival goers, and groups of elderly people, many of whom had come to spend a weekend at the beach and were lining up to take photos with Mar del Plata's emblematic sea lion statue. Everyone moved next to each other, side by side. It seemed like a cinematographic montage made of scenes from totally different movies, ones from different eras and different genres but all filmed in the same location and edited together into a single, long, simultaneous scene. Eventually, I mastered the art of weaving and was able to move smoothly through the crowd, feeling like I was traveling through a collage of parallel realities. Then I spotted a guy with one of those caps with wide and high fronts and disproportionately large bills. I started running faster, hyper focused, as if I were inside a video game, on detecting every guy in the crowd who was wearing one of those caps. I squinted and scanned the multitude. It only took a quick glance to identify which group people belonged to. The cap guys, however, could be found anywhere. They were restricted to no particular group. Well, maybe there weren't any among the elderly. If I were to find a senior citizen wearing one of those hats, it would have unlocked a new level.

An hour later, I was in front of our building again, but before I went in I smoked a cigarette sitting on the railing overlooking the beach. It was still warm, but it had gotten very windy. While some people were on the beach sunbathing in bikinis and shorts, strategically located behind a big rock or a lifeguard tower, others walked around or sat in the sand wearing jackets, jeans, and sneakers. Again, different realities coexisting in the same place. Entire families with baby strollers paraded along the breakwater and took photos at the end of it, standing on top of a rock, off the path, while the waves crashed below them. The ocean seemed to want to sweep them away. I was rooting for the ocean. I was about to leave when a woman caught my attention. She was approaching a couple, asking them something. She wore a long skirt with shiny threads that reflected the sun, a headscarf, and a turquoise shirt, all strong colors but faded, worn out and old. She looked like the girl from the convenience store but without my glasses I couldn't make her out very well. She wasn't the only one. There were several other women just like her, scattered up and down the beach, walking slowly and approaching people. "Oh, *gitanas*!" I thought to myself as if I had solved a great mystery. Before I knew it, she was walking towards me. She was indeed the girl from the convenience store. A little nervous because of her stare, I raised my hand to greet her. She grabbed it.

Drawing in close, she whispered in my ear, "Don't let your smoking habit prevent you from living the good fortune predestined for you." I stayed still, mute.

When she let go of my hand, there was a small, golden horseshoe in it. She remained in front of me, smiling and extending her palm. I understood that she expected a contribution. In the hidden pocket of my running shorts I had forty pesos in ten-peso bills, rolled together, and a separate hundred-peso bill. I considered just giving her ten out of the forty, but I would have had to separate the bills out in front of her and she would have seen that I had more money I wasn't willing to give her. I carefully took out the roll of ten-peso bills, praying that the hundred-peso one wouldn't come out with them. I gave her all the four and consoled myself by thinking that it was less than a pack of cigarettes. Holding the horseshoe tightly in my hand, I stood up quickly, smiled at her, and walked away down the boulevard. I got lost in a kind of *La Salada*-style[7] market, a maze of stalls set up in the sand where sunglasses, sportswear and shorts, shoes, sneakers, flip flops, necklaces, bracelets, and perfumes were all sold. They were counterfeit versions of high-end brands. Or maybe they were actually original but stolen, though the

---

7. La Salada is an illegal street market on the edge of Buenos Aires, where knockoff luxury- and sport-brand products are sold. Its huge. And dangerous. Millions of dollars pass through it every month.

logos looked a little funny. There were even some of those caps with wide bills I kept seeing guys wearing. I bought one, white and black. Thank god I still had the hundred-peso bill.

When I returned to the apartment, the window was wide open. Sunlight flooded every corner and fresh sea breeze/dead fish/salty beach air was circulating. Someone was taking a shower, but I wasn't sure who because no one else was outside the bathroom. On the glass table were the bananas we had bought earlier. I couldn't help but notice that two were missing, although Naty's fruits were still intact and in place, the immaculate apple and her own banana, darker now. There also were dirty cups and plates in the sink. I took off my sneakers and a pile of sand fell to the floor. I set my new cap on my suitcase and put the horseshoe that the fortune teller had given me in my wallet in the same transparent compartment with the acid in its miniscule kitchen plastic-wrap package.

Romina texted me. She had left the cinema and wanted to meet for lunch. I told her I would be ready in no time, but the shower was still running. After grabbing some clothes from my suitcase and laying them out on a chair, I sat on the bed with towels and my hair-styling cream in my lap, staring at the closed bathroom door. Waiting my turn felt like standing in line to pee in a bar bathroom. Or in jail. During the forty minutes I waited, I wondered what a person could be doing in the shower for so long. Maybe she, either Naty or Sol, had OCD like my ex-boyfriend who religiously used to soap himself three times in order to eliminate any germs that might be alive on his skin and wash his hair twice with shampoo and one last time with soap so his hair would be clean. Seriously clean. Or it might have been something more normal. She might have been massaging her scalp for the correct absorption of a capilar treatment mask, removing an ingrown hair in her bikini line, or cleaning under her nails. But the total sum of the time required by each of those activities was way less than what it was actually taking. I was about to knock on the door to see if whoever was in there was still alive. That's when Sol finally came out, emerging from a cloud of steam, like a ghost. The nursery windows immediately fogged up.

"Hi! Did you go for a run? Is it nice out? Is it cold? Is it hot?" she said almost without breathing, her shrill voice sharper than ever. So much steam came off her towel-wrapped body that it seemed like she was on fire.

"Yeah, it's really nice out," I answered, trying to enter the bathroom, but she lingered in the doorway.

"Bikini nice? Or jeans-and-a-T-shirt nice?" she wanted to know, not moving an inch.

"It depends. It's cool in the shade," I explained as I pushed gently past.

I left Sol with her mouth open, confused, her skin still steaming, and I went into the bathroom. It was like being inside a dense cloud. The floor was flooded, the bathmat was soaked, and soap residue mixed with foam had accumulated in the bathtub. I turned on the shower to wash it down the drain, but that made things even worse. A lagoon began to form. The drain was clogged with hair. And more soap. It made me feel sick to touch other people's hair, but it would have been worse to shower in such a disgusting puddle. I pulled, and a tangled ball of blonde hair and tiny bits of soap coated in foam came out. I don't know why I thought of a Christmas tree. I gagged.

Since the hooks to hang towels on were all taken, I turned around to lower the toilet lid so I could leave my things on top of it. That was when I saw it. In the toilet bowl, half inside and half outside the water, there was a kind of poop sticker stuck to the ceramic. I stared at it for several seconds. Had that been the reason Sol had spent so long in the bathroom? Had she left the water running to muffle the noise and take a shit in peace? Mute the splashing and farting sounds? How was she able to shit in conditions that felt like a sauna? It was hot just standing there; I couldn't imagine dealing with it while you were straining to shit. You'd put yourself at risk of fainting. My blood pressure would have plummeted. Or maybe the streak was left over from Naty. That made it even worse because it meant Sol had had no issue coexisting with the shit sticker during the entirety of her eternal shower. Whoever it belonged to might have at least given it a quick pass with the toilet brush, which was sitting right there, next to the toilet. Doing so would have saved me from seeing traces of their shit. A souvenir. It bothered me so much that I decided to use the fancy shampoo and plenty of the imported hair recovery system balsam that one of them had left in there. It smelled so nice. I wondered if they would be able to smell it on me. Maybe not, because I would smell just like them. I regretted the form of my revenge. I had fallen into a trap.

When I got out of the shower, Sol was still in the apartment. She had already put on a lilac dress and a necklace with a very large and pretty transparent violet stone pendant. While I was changing, she went back into the bathroom and brushed her teeth. Then she combed her bangs, first on one side, then on the other, and so on, again and again until she decided on the right side, just like how she'd had them styled since I'd met her. Exactly like Naty's. The last thing she did was put on some red lipstick, little by little, resting the lipstick on her lips, pressing in softly, making dots, then pushing harder, sliding it and joining the dots, until she achieved the intensity she had been looking for. During this process, she told me that Naty had gone for a walk. She said we should all have lunch together.

"I've already made plans to meet Romina for lunch near the cinema," I told her.

"Oh. But Naty wanted to go to the pier," Sol insisted.

I explained to her that we weren't going to be able to join them because we had a movie to go to, and we wouldn't make it in time. We could go another day. Before she could say anything else, I opened the door and left the apartment. She followed me out, but she was silent the whole way down the stairs. The hallways were still chilly, and we were both mute as we left the building. We split up at the corner. I continued along the pedestrian shopping street and she headed to meet Naty.

There were a lot of other people walking in the pedestrian area. The city was indeed full. As I moved between the sportswear and shoe stores, groups of guys wearing caps started appearing. I regretted not wearing mine. I crossed the square at the end of the street and saw Romina sitting outside a cafe, smoking a cigarette with her phone in her hand. She laughed to herself, typing quickly with her fingers. She greeted me without looking up from the screen. Sebastián had been texting her nonstop since midmorning. And she had been answering. But not as herself.

"He thinks I'm Sol," Romina told me, laughing.

He was asking what movies she was going to see. He claimed to be super interested in the film industry and that he would like to attend some of the talks as well. With her.

"You should invite him!" I told her, biting my lips and squinting my eyes, trying to look evil.

"Oh. I mean... Ha! Yeah? Yeah! Hahahaha. You think so?" she wondered out loud while looking at me over her sunglasses.

"Definitely! Think how funny it would be. We should properly organize it though." I tried to imagine the confusion we could generate. We both burst out laughing, and while I was drying the tears of evil childish joy running down my cheeks I remembered that we needed to send a message to Sol and Naty so we could have lunch together.

"Ah, right," Romina sighed. "Naty tried to convince me to go to the pier. I told her we couldn't, that they could join us here if they wanted. She said okay, but that they were far away so it would take a while for them to get here."

We asked the waitress to set two extra places because we

were waiting for more people, though Romina and I were starving so we went ahead and ordered two salads and a bottle of red wine. When Naty and Sol arrived, over an hour later, we had already finished eating and were working on our last glasses of wine. They sat at the places that had been set for them, but Naty was cold and Sol said the wi-fi signal was too weak. We moved inside.

Naty asked the waitress if she could bring something other than butter. She wanted something else to accompany the tiny basket of complementary toast. A moment later, another waitress came with a plate of pickled eggplants.

Before she could set it down, Naty said, "They're free, right? 'Cause you need to offer other options besides just butter."

The waitress nodded. I thought I saw her roll her eyes, but maybe that was just me. Naty stabbed at some of the eggplant with her fork, but when she realized she'd speared a whole slice, she put it back down and asked Sol to cut it up for her, claiming it was too big to fit on top of one of the tiny pieces of toast. Without saying a word, Sol cut the eggplant slice into smaller pieces. Naty insisted the pieces were still too big and that Sol cut them again. Then again. Each time, Sol was mute and expressionless. When Naty finally found them to be an acceptable size, she took a piece and placed it on top of one of the tiny pieces of toast. She brought the toast to her wide-open mouth, but she didn't take a bite. She said she couldn't eat it. She was still too anxious. Something horrible had happened to her during her morning walk.

I thought maybe the wind had messed up her bangs or she had broken a nail. Romina must have been thinking the same thing. She was desperately trying to make eye contact with me, and I had to force myself to avoid her gaze so as not to burst into laughter.

"I already know the story. It's so creepy," Sol said. "Tell the girls, Naty, tell them. It's so creepy."

Naty's eyes were fixed on the little piece of eggplant toast she was unable to eat. She had it in her fingers, still hanging in the air, almost to her mouth. After Sol finished arranging the remainder of the cut-up pieces of eggplant according to Naty's liking, she placed her hand on her shoulder. But Naty remained quiet, as did the rest of us. The general silence, dramatic but with a lack of any tension, persisted a few moments until Romina broke it.

"So, what happened?"she asked, glancing over at me.

"Okay, okay. So, this morning, I was walking, super chill, along the sea path, and at one point I went down to the beach because I wanted to feel the sand on my feet. Suddenly, a *gitana* approached me. I have no idea where she came from. She wanted to give me a palm reading. I told her like thirty times that I wasn't interested, but she kept following me around, insisting. Then she yelled at me: 'Hey, big eyes! Look at me, let me see your fortune." And I didn't do anything because I was afraid that she would, like—I don't know—rob me? And also I was, like, disgusted, you know? She was all dirty and smelly. So I started walking faster to leave her behind. I was sure I had, but after a while, when I sat down to rest, she appeared in front of me again and—I have no idea how—she grabbed my hand and looked into my eyes."

"She asked me about my Antonio Banderas," Naty said, her voice turning sweet and tender. She loosened her shoulders and leaned back in her chair, finally putting the toast in her mouth. "I thought it was funny, not because I need a gypsy to help me get him, but I told her about the film director I'm into, and she told me that we were going to have three children—two of them would be twins—that we were going to get married when I turn thirty-two years old—that is, in four years—and that we're going to live in another city." She smiled widely. Then she paused and looked straight at Romina and me. She explained that Victor, the film director, had always told her he wanted to move to London. At that moment, I felt warmth in my heart, warmth for the story Naty had playing in her head, for her tenderness. I don't know, it moved me. She was so in love with that Victor guy. I imagined her sitting on the beach, alone, her hopes buoyed by the *gitana*'s words.

"And then what happened?" Romina asked, sipping the last of the wine from her glass.

"I kept looking at her, and she smiled at me," Naty said. Then, suddenly, she changed the tone of her voice and started speaking faster, almost without pausing, escalating in volume and emotion. "Then—that bitch—she grabbed my hand tighter and extended the other one to me and told me, 'A donation, please.' And I realized that she'd fooled me. It was all a scam. She'd just buttered me up to get money from me. So I just gave her a two-peso coin I had in my pocket. But she told me, 'No coins: they're bad luck,' so I gave her a two-peso bill. But she wouldn't let me go and asked me for more. I didn't want to give her more. What did she want, like twenty pesos? I mean, like, what?" She sighed, took a deep breath and continued. "Then, she told me to put down another bill to form a cross so that everything she had predicted would come true. Ha. I wasn't going to fall for that, and I wasn't going to give her anything else. It's not like I was carrying that much cash anyway, and, hey, two pesos was fine. So I started to pull my hand away, but she wouldn't let go. So I got up and kept pulling until I broke away and she fell down, hard, to the ground. I'd used all the strength I had to free myself. All her fortune teller friends who were nearby turned toward us and started walking over. I panicked. I tried to leave but they blocked my way, making a circle around me. One of them even pulled my hair! I hugged my bag. I panicked! I was surrounded! They asked me for my watch. They said it was old, that I could buy another one. Then they asked for my earrings, then my necklace. I started bitching them out, and then the woman I had thrown to the floor—ugh, all ugly and dirty. I'll never forget that face. I swear I never will—she shouted at me, 'May you find an avalanche of shit in a dead-end alley.' What a disgusting bitch. How could she say that to me? Then I realized they were all barefoot and I stomped on somebody's foot, and that's how I was able to make some room to escape."

Romina said she would have told them to read her palm while she stuck her middle finger in the air, and Sol said that she'd already told her that she was too softhearted and innocent for paying the lady any attention in the first place. I wanted to tell her what had happened to me and that if she had just handed over another twenty pesos she would have put an end to the matter and been able to keep enjoying the beach.

I started saying, "Maybe if you had given her some more money…"

But she interrupted me and said, "Why? Why should I have to give them any money? They're all dirty thieves," and, "You weren't there so you don't know how you would have reacted."

Dirty thieves or not, Naty was a fucking cheapskate, I thought. But, again, I wasn't anywhere near close enough with her to tell her how ridiculously mean and cheap she was. Two pesos. You couldn't even buy a kitchen rag for two pesos. I didn't tell the story of my own encounter. Something in her tone when she'd answered me had infuriated me. I stared into her eyes and asked if she had returned the curse.

"What?" she responded, opening her already-big eyes even wider.

"Well, she definitely cursed you. Did you curse her back?" I said, moving my fork around in the air to emphasize my speech. "Because if not, the curse stays with you." I paused dramatically, and then, pointing my fork directly at her, I asked, "Didn't you know that?"

Naty looked at me like I was talking about quantum physics. Her eyes grew increasingly wide. For a second, I thought they were going to fall from their sockets. She reminded me of a cartoon character, though I couldn't remember which.

"Look," I said, "I don't believe in any of this mystical shit, but my grandmother, she was from Romania and she knows all about *gitanas* and curses and that stuff. She's also, like, half witch or has like a sixth sense or something. One time she told me that if you ever get cursed, you have to curse the person back. That way, because they're really superstitious, they'll remove the curse from you. Otherwise, it stays with you forever."

"Well, I curse her back. Let an avalanche of shit fall on *her*. No, even better, I curse her to sink in a pond of shit," she said, throwing what was left of the tiny toast on the plate.

"Hmm. No, no, no. You don't understand. It has to be right at the moment, looking straight into her eyes. Now, here, between us, it has no effect." I explained this very calmly, acting like an expert on curses.

"So, what? Do I have to go look for her?" she said, challenging my wisdom.

"Well, I don't know what to tell you. Do whatever you want. Me, I'm afraid of them. Today, I also came across a group and avoided them completely. Maybe it's just a story. You know what old ladies are like."

Realizing we were going to be late for our movie, Romina interrupted the dialogue. We asked for our bill and paid. We stood up at the exact moment Naty and Sol's food arrived. Sol had ordered a burger that was bigger than her head. She struggled to grab it properly, trying different approaches, but her hands were too small, and she couldn't lift it without things falling out. Faced with the imminent risk of the whole thing breaking into pieces, she ended up leaning over her plate and taking small bites. Naty regretted having ordered one dish each. It was too much food, she said. Of course, it was also cheaper to share. Then she complained that the vegetables in the side dish that came with her grilled chicken breast, which looked like a tic-tac-toe board made on unbelievably white meat, were too big. Sol told her that they weren't and that she should just eat them.

While we were walking towards the cinema, Romina

asked me if everything I had said about the curses was true. I told her it was total bullshit.

"My grandmother was Italian, and she died before I was born. I never even met the woman. I heard she was tiny and super mean, though."

That afternoon, we watched three movies, one after the other. We had about 20 minutes between the first and second, and we thought it would be enough time to grab a few beers. We ran to the Chinese supermarket around the corner and bought several ice-cold cans, which we hid under a sweatshirt in Romina's backpack so they wouldn't be confiscated while entering the screening, but the checkout line was so long we were late getting back to the cinema. We ended up in the front row with our necks craned backwards, turning our heads from side to side in order to see the full screen and follow the subtitles.

The movie had been entirely filmed in Mexico, and the last scene, when the protagonist got on the subway, took me back in time to my last stay in Mexico City, a few months previous. The protagonist took the same line that I took every day to get to the house I was staying in. He even used the same station. I spaced out during the end of the movie, lost in my thoughts, reliving moments in the Bosque de Chapultepec, the smell of the food stalls, the taste of the taquitos and beer from the little corner bar.

When the lights came on, the director stood right in front of us and introduced himself. He was Mexican, a big guy with shiny, abundant, dark hair, a soap opera heartthrob who spoke softly and sweetly with a noticeable accent. It was astonishing that he was also wearing one of those big caps. Once again, I regretted not having brought mine. Romina and I stayed in our front-row seats like there wasn't a panel discussion about the film happening around us, cracking open cans of beer and sipping them shamelessly. We didn't ask any questions, but it seemed like a fine place to wait for the start of the next movie, which was being shown in the same cinema complex. I found myself listening closely to everything the Mexican was saying. It was all very interesting: the story that had inspired him, how he had managed to raise funds to make the film, and the obstacles he had to overcome. It was admirable and encouraging. The way he explained his work, step by step, made it all seem very achievable. Maybe I could also film a movie and show it at festivals. It wasn't a bad idea. I was sure I could get funds somehow. I was focused, already elaborating a plan, when his crotch caught my eye. His fly was down. Now it was all I could think about. He was right in front of us, and I was sure that if I told Romina about it, even if I whispered, he would have heard. I pondered whether it was a good idea to tell him, to signal him in some discreet way so as not to embarrass him in front of the whole crowd, but I was afraid that once he became aware of his situation, he might lose all confidence in himself and his work. He could develop a traumatic fear of public speaking and never lecture in front of an audience ever again. Would he be able to film another movie after that? It could mean the end of his career. I could see his red underwear clearly, the tight fabric peeking out of the open zipper. I was sure they were briefs. If they had been boxers, the fabric would have been wrinkled. Or maybe they were boxers and his dick was so big that it was stretching the fabric out. I turned around. The cinema was full. Was I the only one who had noticed? People raised their hands and asked very specific questions about the film. The whole brief-boxer-big dick thing started making me anxious, and I told Romina I was going to the bathroom and that I'd wait for her outside. While I peed, my ass and thighs hovering over the toilet seat so as not to let it come into contact with my skin, I realized that at some point, after the talk was over, he would finally realize that his fly had been down the whole time. By then, it would be too late for me to do anything about it. I hoped it wouldn't be too terrible for him. I loved Mexico and Mexicans very much. And he seemed so nice. Such a hardworking and engaged artist.

Because there were still a few minutes before the next movie, I left the bathroom and looked for the closest exit. I wanted to smoke a cigarette. I had a strange feeling as I walked through the shopping mall where the cinema complex was. Going down the escalators, I spotted a Freddo ice cream shop on one of the floors and was struck by a strange sensation of familiarity, the kind of nostalgia you get when you've been away from your own country for a long time and you suddenly come across something that reminds you of it. It hit me unexpectedly and left me confused and dizzy as I kept descending toward the ground floor.

Once outside, I saw a Garbarino store across the street, and I was struck again with the same Freddo sensation, but stronger this time. It was the second blow of nostalgia in a row, and I'd had no idea that Garbarino was expanding internationally. The feeling grew. I was completely overcome with nostalgia and dizziness and confusion until I remembered that I was in Mar Del Plata, near Buenos Aires, Argentina, not in Mexico. I laughed and choked on the cigarette smoke.

I was 100-percent back in Argentina and halfway through my cigarette when Romina appeared out of nowhere, shouting, "We have to run!"

She took hold of my hand and dragged me along with her, moving quickly. I thought maybe the cinema people were after us because of the beers. Or that the Mexican guy was mad I hadn't spoken up about his zipper. But it was just that Romina had made a mistake. The next movie wasn't in the same theater complex, and we had to move. We were already late. Again. Halfway there, we realized that we'd been looking at the map upside down, and we turned around and started running the other way.

The movie had already started, and once more we ended up in the front row. All that wine and beer had left me sleepy and more than a bit tipsy. At first, I thought my drunkenness was the reason I was unable to follow the plot, but soon I realized the film was just a succession of short videos of cities that the director, a Russian this time, had visited, with somewhat inspiring quotes or anecdotal phrases, narrated in Russian by a neutral female voice. The Spanish subtitles were in yellow, placed over white English subtitles. This made it even more difficult to focus. I was fighting to both not go crosseyed and to keep my eyes open when I read, "The day is long, but life is short." I gave up and fell asleep, totally convinced that if someone had gotten money to do that shit then I could definitely get some too. Romina woke me up several times, first because I was snoring, then to give me a free sample of a lemon cookie that she had gotten earlier in the pedestrian zone. It wasn't covered in chocolate, which was disappointing. The final time she woke me up was so we could leave, long before the movie ended.

We returned to the house on foot. Romina said that there was nothing to worry about. We still had some beers in her backpack. Though warm, they felt fine.

Naty and Sol weren't there when we arrived, but I saw that the bananas had multiplied and new tangerines had been born.

"They replaced the bananas they ate this morning," I pointed out to Romina, amazed.

"I don't understand why Naty doesn't eat the one she brought," she said.

"Because it went so bad that you couldn't even make banana bread with it anymore. But she won't throw it away either. Have you seen the pile of dirty dishes and cups in the sink?"

I couldn't stand seeing dirty dishes. Especially if they weren't my dirty dishes.

"Yeah, but the thing is that there's no dish soap. Sol told me this morning," Romina explained, sort of defending them, which made me angry.

I went to check. I found soap, a sponge, and several

other cleaning supplies under the counter. I left them out so they'd realized they could wash their things. Romina and I were hungry, and out of habit I opened the refrigerator. I found a container. It held almost the entire hamburger Sol had ordered at lunch. Almost certainly, the idea of taking the leftovers had been Naty's. We saw that there were still some fries, which didn't even last long enough to be reheated. We ate them from the container, standing in front of the open fridge. Romina wondered where Naty's leftovers were.

"Probably in the trash," I told her. "That chicken looked awful."

We both had our doubts, knowing that Naty would never waste a cent. We ate practically all of the leftovers, only leaving a part of the hamburger that was kind of wet. When we were done, we decided to throw everything in the trash and take it out to the can in the hallway, destroying the evidence.

"It'll be like nothing happened, like the burger was never even there," Romina said.

After a while we started craving something sweet. The immaculate apple was still there, but it wasn't that appealing to either of us now. We remembered Sol's tangerine cake. We found the Tupperware container among Sol's stuff. There was a lot left. We ate it all except for one extremely thin slice, the width of a piece of American cheese, which we only left so they wouldn't be able to say we'd eaten everything. It stood there, alone, the tiny slice of cake in the exact middle of the Tupperware, which we closed and put back where we'd found it.

The girls still hadn't come back by the time we went to bed. Romina was convinced that they had gone to some party without inviting us. Naty's attitude bothered her, and she fired off a verbal list of everything she was upset by. I agreed with everything, and, perhaps to stoke her anger a little more, I told her about the shit sticker I had found in the morning. Romina was outraged, especially because the apartment had to be left more or less clean if she wanted to get her 300-peso cash deposit back. At some point, while we were talking, we fell asleep.

At dawn, an alarm rang. The sound was coming from Romina's backpack, but she slept right through it, giving no sign or movement indicating discomfort as a result of the insistent, annoying ringing. The depth of Romina's sleep was unbelievable. It's probably why she was always late for work. The alarm turned off on its own and then started ringing again.

The fourth time this happened, Naty furiously shouted from her room, "The alarm!"

Romina woke up at once, doing her weird little possessed jump again, which left her sitting upright on the bed with a disoriented expression, not knowing where she was or what was happening.

"Your alarm clock has been ringing for a thousand years," I told her.

"Ugh. Today is Monday. I forgot to turn it off," she said, digging for it in her backpack.

Romina managed to stop the alarm and immediately turned over and went back to sleep. I tried to do the same, but in between dreams I heard Naty get up to go to the toilet several times.

A few hours later, Romina got up because she had a movie. I went down to open the door for her then went for a run. I listened to electronic music, the rhythm of which gave me the energy to cover the kilometers necessary to reach the lighthouse. This time, I wore my new cap, and when I passed someone else with a cap, we would inevitably exchange glances and a wink, as if we belonged to some Mar del Plata gang. It made me feel powerful and I ran faster and faster.

When I returned, I sat on the beach railing again. There were a lot more people than there had been the day before, probably because the weather was warmer. There was no sign of the *gitanas*.

Before going back up to the apartment, I stopped by the convenience store for a Coke. Big Boobs was at the window. I wondered if she ever had a day off. The side door was open, so I went in. There were a couple of people in line in front of me. A tall man was working the counter, his black hair combed back with so much gel it looked like a large animal had licked his hair into place. His arms were covered in leather bracelets up to the elbows. While waiting my turn, I stared at a colorful scarf hanging from one of the shelves. It had the faded tone of the fortune teller girl's clothes. I asked for the Coke, but I didn't have a chance to inquire about her. He was unfriendly. Before I had even paid, he was already calling the next person in line. Maybe he was in a competition against the big boobs girl to see who could serve more people per hour or something. I left the convenience store annoyed and somewhat confused.

Sol was startled when I entered the apartment, like I had caught her doing something forbidden. But she was just sitting on the floor, arranging some paper bags in her luggage. She put everything inside her backpack and got up quickly. At first, I thought Naty wasn't there, but then I heard her voice calling for Sol from the bathroom. Sol went in and closed the door behind her. I sat on one of the red vintage chairs to drink my Coke. I stared at the bathroom door and the light coming through the glass bricks. There was a murmur of voices, but I couldn't make out what they were saying. My mind went blank. I couldn't imagine what they might be doing in there. When the door opened, only Sol emerged. Very slowly, she closed the door behind her. She stood and looked at me for a few minutes. When the sound of the running shower started, she explained to me, almost whispering, that Naty was not well. I looked at her, waiting for further information. Obviously she hadn't told me enough for me to understand what was happening. She put her ear to the door, then walked over to me. She grabbed my hand and repeated that Naty was not well. She said it over and over again. A broken record. I wanted to tap her on the head to help her ideas get unstuck so she could move forward to the next thought, but luckily such measures weren't necessary. She continued her explanation, saying that Naty was very scared. Sol had been trying to calm her down. The whole fortune teller thing had traumatized her. Naty was fully convinced that she had indeed been cursed.

"She woke up with stomach cramps and diarrhea, and she's been on the toilet ever since. Poor thing. She was crying. I hugged her and held her hand for a while so that she didn't feel alone."

I instantly let go of Sol's hand and went to the kitchen sink. I acted like I was getting a glass of water, but really I was scrubbing my hands. Sol had held Naty's hand while she was taking a shit. Did Naty think the toilet was going to swallow her? My mental image was something like the scene of a childbirth, Naty squeezing her hand and pushing and Sol modeling deep breaths so that Naty could expel everything inside of her. I wanted to laugh as much as I wanted to run away. Dirty dishes had continued to pile up in the kitchen, except for the Tupperware, which had been washed and leaned against the wall to dry. I wondered who had eaten the thin slice of cake. Sol or Naty?

Naty left the bathroom and came straight into the kitchen to talk to me. She stood in the door and in a post-diarrhea voice that was at once weak and furious, she demanded I tell her everything I knew about *gitanas*. I explained that I'd already told her everything I knew. She asked me to call my grandmother and get more information. When I told her that my grandma was dead, Naty crumpled the floor.

She told me that she had gone out in the morning to look for the fortune tellers in order to confront them and curse them back, as I'd instructed, but they were nowhere to be found. It was as if they had disappeared. From the floor, she looked up at me with her bulging eyes, which were sad and desperate and had dark circles under them. She was blocking my exit. To rid myself of her, I said she'd probably find them later—maybe she should even try now, since it was already past noon. She got up in slow motion, then told Sol to hurry up. Sol was also on the floor, rummaging around in the paper bags in her backpack. They both left without even combing their bangs or putting on lipstick.

Romina and I arranged to meet at the fisherman's pier for lunch. I laughed to myself on the way over. I couldn't wait to tell her everything about Naty and Sol, but when I got to the pier, I saw Sol standing besides Romina, leaning against a railing. She was carrying a big shopping bag. Before I could ask about her whereabouts, Sol told me that Naty would be arriving later. I asked if they had found the *gitanas*. They hadn't, but they had spent a lot of time walking around looking for them. Sol said that at one point she was exhausted and went into a store to buy some things, and Naty, who thought she'd seen someone she knew walk by, disappeared while she was paying. After that, Sol didn't catch up with her again.

"But she messaged me that she'd have lunch with us," Sol clarified.

I imagined Naty desperately looking for the *gitanas* amongst all the people sunbathing on the beach while the three of us walked together along the pier to the restaurant. The dining room was paneled in dark wood, and a chorus of creaks, a murmur as soft as background music, could be heard, as if the walls were talking behind our backs. Inside, everything seemed suspended, slowed down by the dense, salty, sticky air. The smudged windows looked like portholes from an old ship. Since the restaurant was on the very end of the pier, we were surrounded by water, and it felt like we were on the high seas. An old-school waiter served us. He was tall and fat and in a terrible mood. He wore the traditional uniform (black pants, a white dress shirt, and a bowtie) sadly and sloppily. He brought us a bread basket, and we only ordered drinks because Sol said we should wait for Naty to order food. Romina asked for a bottle of wine. Sol and I ordered a liter of beer to share.

Sol placed the big shopping bag she was carrying on the table. Inside it were the same sort of smaller paper bags I had seen her stuffing into her backpack earlier. I asked what they were.

"Oh, just some souvenirs I bought," she answered, a bit shy, but excited too.

"Can I take a look at them?"

She reluctantly agreed. I stretched out my hand for her to hand me the bag. Instead, she put the bag in her lap and moved aside her plate and her glass, clearing a space in front of her on the table. Then, slowly, almost ceremonially, she opened each paper bag and took out the souvenirs, one by one. They were little plastic figurines that changed color depending on the weather, different sizes and shapes. There was a large sea lion, two small ones, a Virgin of Luján, a little fishing boat, a lighthouse, and so on. She placed them side by side in a perfect row, facing her.

"Aren't they super cute?" She looked at them with fascination, her palms open.

"Yes. They are super cute. My grandmother has an antique one, made of glass," I told her.

"Your grandmother from Romania? Isn't she dead?" Sol asked, staring into my eyes, almost defiantly.

"No, not that one. The other one," I told her, though it had been a gift from one grandmother to the other.

"Who did you buy them for?" Romina wanted to know. She sipped her second glass of wine.

"No, not for anyone. They're for me, for my new house. I want to line them up in the kitchen window."

"Oh," Romina and I said at the same time.

"I bought some others yesterday. Some are the same; some are different. I love them. I've been seeing them in the shop windows, all in a row." She sighed. "In the store they were all purple, but now they're changing. They're turning blue," she added, a little worried.

"Blue is nice weather, violet is variable, pink is rain," I told her, not because I knew, but because it said so on the stickers stuck to the bottoms of the souvenirs.

"Yes, I like good weather, but they're prettier when they're purple. I like purple. They're almost always purple in the shop windows." She was grinning enthusiastically.

"Well, it's a question of temperature and humidity. Since the liquid inside is sensitive to those factors, they change color depending on the air temperature and conditions. Maybe the air conditioning in the stores turns them purple, and, once outside in the open air, they turn blue," Romina commented, surprising me with her scientific knowledge.

Sol, whose eyes had been fixed on her collection, looked up and sighed thoughtfully. After another moment of contemplation, she returned them to their paper bags. She closed the shopping bag and got up to go to the bathroom. Romina and I watched her in silence as she walked away from us and disappeared behind the bar.

"She should put them in the bathroom so when they change color she'll realize how long she's been in there," I said.

"Ha. You're mean," she replied. "Although it is kind of strange to buy so many souvenirs for the kitchen. One would be plenty."

"It's super fucking weird. Hey, and Naty? Did Sol tell you about Naty's breakdown? She held Naty's hand in the bathroom while she was taking a shit." I told her, updating her..

"What? Shut up! No!" Romina exclaimed, doubting the extremely bizarre piece of information I had provided.

"No, seriously. I'm telling you! Naty got explosive diarrhea, probably from eating the bowl full of bananas and tangerines, but she's certain it has something to do with the fortune tellers. She really thinks she's cursed. So she had a mental breakdown while shitting, and Sol went into the bathroom so she wouldn't feel alone and held her hand as she expelled her never-ending liquid shit. And she was crying, afraid the avalanche-of-shit curse was starting to take effect."

"What? Are you serious? Really?" she said, still skeptical. "The last time we traveled together they were a little weird, but not this weird. This is all fucking weird"

We didn't have time to discuss the matter further. Naty had entered the restaurant and was walking towards us. Her constipated bitch face looked more constipated and bitchier than ever. Even the explosive diarrhea she had had all morning hadn't gotten rid of it. Naty wasn't alone. A tall guy, wearing a plaid shirt and jeans, walked beside and slightly behind her. He had buzzed hair, which we were able to see once he reached our table and took off his cap, a big one, like the ones I kept seeing everywhere, like the one I had bought.

"This is Juan. This is Romina and... Romina's friend," she said, pointing at us and sitting at the table.

"Carolina. Hello." I shook his hand.

"Hello." He greeted us both with a kiss, making smacking sounds against our cheeks, and sat at the head of the table.

He was really good looking, super hot in a way similar to Chino Darín[8]. He had a hoarse voice that vibrated and made everything go out of focus each time he spoke. Despite his manly posturing, he seemed shy. I offered him some beer.

"He doesn't drink beer, and he is not going to eat either. He's just here to keep me company for a while," Naty said.

"Maybe some wine?" Romina offered.

Naty answered for him before he had a chance to respond.

"No, he doesn't drink alcohol."

"But you wear a cap. Everyone wears a cap here," I told him.

"Yes, but his is original. See? He has the sticker that

---

8. Chino Darín is the son of the amazing Argentine actor Ricardo Darín. They are both very, very hot.

proves it's original." Once again, she answered before Juan could say anything. She pointed to a big round metallic sticker on the bill.

"So you left the sticker on?" Romina asked.

"Of course he did. That way everyone knows it's original and not from La Salada," Naty interrupted again. Then she turned to Juan and pointed at me. "She bought one at that lousy market on the beach. It's so fake it hurts your eyes."

Sol came back from the toilet.

"Hiiiiii," she exclaimed in a high-pitched voice while waving with her tiny hands.

She sat and quickly checked on her paper bags. Naty continued to act like Juan's agent or interpreter, giving answers to questions. Juan didn't look up from his phone, but she treated him affectionately, batting her eyelashes, reaching out to touch his leg or his hand, and speaking in what seemed to be some sort of private code. At one point, his phone rang, and he announced that he was leaving. He said a goodbye to everyone, no *mwah* kiss this time, but just a little wave directed at the group. Naty's eyes followed him as he walked across the dining room and out the door, her head rested on her folded arms.

"Isn't he so, so cute?" Naty asked. "He was obviously nervous."

"Really? I didn't notice. How come?" Romina asked, confused.

"Well, he always is when he's in public. He doesn't like to be recognized."

I was intrigued—and I imagined Romina was too—by the mystery and enigma Naty had planted, wrapped in a mixture of thirst for gossip and curiosity about what weird shit she would come up with next. But our primary motivation was the sensation of hunger, and our attention turned to the waiter, who was getting ready to bring over our dishes, so nobody asked what it was we might recognize him from. Regardless, Naty explained that he was an actor in a soap opera that aired on national TV at two in the afternoon. Sol nodded, bobbing her head up and down so many times it seemed as if she had forgotten how to make any other movement. Romina and I had never heard of him or of the soap opera.

The waiter arrived. Our plates overflowed with pleasure and happiness, except for Naty's. She had ordered grilled fish with a boiled potato. The large "Don Luis" haddock skewer covered with a mustard cream and the salmon with black butter and caper sauce each looked like a feast in themselves. Naty couldn't turn her bulging eyes away from my Provençal mussels, which were gigantic, almost mutant, in size. She suggested, with a falsely sweet voice, like she would be doing me a big favor, that I take half her grilled fish and boiled potato in exchange for half of my mussels. I politely refused, thanking her for the kind offer and telling her to help herself to some of my mussels. I called the waiter to order a side of fries, an essential accompaniment to the exquisite flavor of that amazing, fresh seafood.

We were so delighted with the food, the wine, the beer, and the feeling of the high seas that when Romina and I finally checked the time, we realized that we were going to be late again. The most efficient thing seemed to be to leave the money for our share of the bill and let the girls finish eating in peace. Then, when they were ready to leave, they could pay for everything together. I did some mental math and left my share, as well as Romina's, on the table. We would settle it up between us later. Romina had drunk a whole bottle of wine and was having a hard time concentrating. But Naty called the waiter and asked for the bill.

"I didn't drink wine or beer, so we have to divide the ticket carefully," she said, pushing away the pile of cash that I had left in the center of the table.

She was such a cheapskate she thought we were going to fuck her over. The desire to fight with her welled up inside of me, but it was pointless. The waiter brought the bill, and Naty wanted to kill herself when she realized that by ordering a main dish with a side she ended up having to pay much more than any of the rest of us who had ordered beers and wine and delicious food from the list of daily specials. It turned out that I had left more than our fair share, so I recovered some of the money from the pile. As we were leaving, I heard her ask the waiter to bring the cap to her small bottle of water so she could take it with her to finish later.

Romina and I spent the entire afternoon inside movie theaters. Afterwards, Romina made me walk around the downtown area searching for her favorite churro place. She bought three with *dulce de leche* filling. Then we stopped in Havanna and bought two coffees to go, one with white chocolate and one with hazelnuts. The cream on top was so high that we didn't want to crush it with the lids. It looked so nice. A sweet cloud.

We sat on the beach with our coffees. Romina was dunking her churros. The sun was going down, and it was quite windy, but it was pleasant. While I used a stir stick to scoop out the cream and sugar that remained in the bottom of my cup, licking it like it was the most delicious thing on earth, and Romina was dipping her last churro, a dog approached, wagging his tail. He circled us a few times and then lay down in front of us. He was just chilling, smiling like only a dog can smile, and he watched us with sweet eyes. Then suddenly, he would transform into our guardian, barking and growling at absolutely any person or animal that came within a five-meter radius.

"He would have helped Naty with the *gitanas*," I told Romina.

"He would have bitten Naty," she answered, cackling.

"But Sol would have made a circle of protection around her with all the souvenirs she's been buying," I said.

"Ohhh, and she would have done a rain dance, or a cloud dance, so they'd turn violet instead of blue" she added, cracking up.

"I want to become better friends with her, so she invites

me to her house. I want to see them all lined up in the kitchen window," I continued, holding my stomach, already convulsing with laughter.

"Will you hold her hand while she poops?" Romina said, barely able to finish the sentence.

We kept imagining thousands of scenarios, but we couldn't manage to put them into words. Just by beginning to talk about them, we ended up laughing so much that our guard dog turned on us, baring his teeth and barking at us to stop, so we decided to leave and go take a nap.

We fell asleep watching a *Simpsons* marathon. When Naty and Sol entered the apartment, the television was still on and we were both still lying in bed. Romina was fast asleep. I was dozing on and off. They didn't care. They slammed the door, turned on the lights, and dragged the chairs around.

"Oh hi," I said, not moving from the bed, "I didn't hear you come in."

They just looked at me without answering. They sat down at the table, eating tangerines and bananas. I was trying to figure out which bananas were theirs and which ones were mine when Romina asked them about the movies they had seen. I stayed quiet and kept my eyes on the TV. *The Simpsons* had ended and an episode of a TV show that I had seen only once had begun. It was about a group of girls who lived in a sorority house at an elite university in the United States. The leader was blonde and very pretty, always dressed in pink, and wore a lot of makeup. In order to continue existing as a sorority, the university was forcing them to accept more members. The new ones they had been able to recruit were, in the opinion of the blonde leader, fat and uncool, but everyone else loved them and she couldn't stand it. Everything was exaggerated and very grotesque. Meanwhile, there was a murderer on the loose, killing them one by one in the strangest ways. The leader also had a hidden room in the house that was full of all sorts of knives. Her boyfriend was the hottest boy on campus, but he was cheating on her with someone else. His lover was turned on by death, so she always took him to the cemetery to fuck. Because Naty, Sol, and Romina were talking so loudly, I couldn't hear the dialogue, but I was able to follow the story through the images and subtitles until Naty started doing yoga exercises in front of the TV. I could only see intermittently through the spaces between Naty's arms, legs, and head. When the sorority girls started screaming in fear because they had found a dead girl in the bathroom, Naty stood, blocking the entire screen. She turned it off, saying that the volume was bothering her. She turned and walked past my bed in the direction of the nursery, staring at me defiantly, as if expecting me to say something.

But I didn't have to say anything.

Her whole attitude of owning and controlling the world just because she could turn off the TV without asking, without even caring, was gone in less than a second.

She let out a long, endless, super loud fart.

Or rather, a long, endless, super loud fart escaped from her. She put one hand on her belly and the other on her mouth. The farting situation was obviously out of her control. It went on, purring almost, stable and continuous. Embarrassed, she quickened her pace, but that only made it worse, and the noise grew louder. We all suspected the worst, but only Romina said it.

"Did you just shit yourself, Naty?" she said, loud and clear.

Naty started yelling at Romina that it wasn't funny, that she had an upset stomach.

"But Naty, woman, go into the bathroom or outside or something. Now it smells horrible in here. And you should stop eating tangerines and bananas if you don't want to shit yourself anymore," said Romina very seriously.

Sol stayed still, and I covered half my face with the blanket so she wouldn't notice that I was holding back a deformed laugh. Naty yelled at Romina, saying how insensitive she was, how hurt she felt. Instead of asking her for forgiveness, Romina also started cracking up, Naty began to insult her. Slowly, Sol crept into the nursery and opened the window. Naty continued screaming from the nursery, the redness in her face still visible through the fake window. When Sol came back out, Naty slammed the door so hard it rattled the glass. She paced back and forth, talking to herself.

"Sure, close the door. Don't worry about us. We're just going to suffocate in your shit smell," Romina said indignantly, but she was still chuckling.

She got up and tried to open the door, but Naty had closed it so hard that it had gotten stuck, and they started shouting at each other through the glass. Sol had become frozen again. The shouting was becoming more and more unbearably hellish, just like the smell of shit that was floating, invading, dominating every single air molecule. Without saying a word, I put on my shoes and left the apartment.

Once outside, I took a deep breath and closed my eyes. An icy, salty aura of freshness invaded my nostrils, almost burning them. Despite the slightest hint of a fishy smell, it was a purifying experience. I walked along the pedestrian street for a while. It was windy, and leaves were swirling in the air. Pedestrians' scarves flapped like flags and their hair went from one side of their heads to the other, sometimes covering their faces. I reached the corner and was about to enter a sports store when I saw the fluttering of a colorful faded scarf. I started walking faster, dodging people without taking my eyes off it. I'd occasionally lose sight of it until it popped back up in the air. I walked several blocks, moving faster and faster. I was getting closer. Just as I was about to reach it, I got something in my eye. I tried to blink it away, but I had to stop because it hurt and wouldn't come out. I entered a coffee shop and went straight to the restrooms to splash some water in my eye. After a few minutes, I managed to get rid of whatever it was, but my eye was all red, itchy, and irritated. When I came out of the toilet, I saw through the cafe's windows that it had started to rain pretty hard. I sat at a table and ordered a cappuccino. The rain didn't fall in any particular direction. The wind swung the mass of water and people tried to cover themselves as best they could. Umbrellas, destroyed in seconds, were of no use. When I had just about finished my cappuccino, my phone buzzed. It was a message from the Thrush.

"Hey lady. I tried them last night. Fuck, it was an unbelievable *mambo*! Have you already taken them?"

"No. The only *mambo* going on here is that these girls are all crazy," I replied.

"Uh, Caro, little ladies traveling together always equals mess."

I saw my reflection in the window, sitting there with my giant cappuccino cup, surrounded by a bunch of old people sipping tea and coffee. I asked for the check. While I was looking for my money, I checked the little compartment in my wallet where I'd put the acid. The tabs were still there, packed in tight with the horseshoe the *gitana* had given me, as if they had become BFFs, Naty and Sol style. I didn't wait for my change. I went across the street to a Chinese supermarket where I bought two bottles of wine. The fierce rain had slowed to a drizzle so faint that it was almost invisible and made me doubt whether it was real or just a phantom sensation, although there was enough of it to moisten my face and slightly wet my clothes, annoying and confusing me like anything that it is but it is not, fake but real. The wind was still quite strong though. As I walked back to the apartment, I felt like I was in an epic scene from a movie about the end of the world.

I was curious and a little afraid of what I might find when I opened the apartment door. Luckily, the vibe had changed. Not only was the smell gone, but everyone seemed calm and quiet. They were all doing their own thing, Sol with her souvenirs, Romina in bed scrolling her phone, and Naty in the bathroom.

I said, "Hi" almost silently and went to the kitchen to open the wine and look for some glasses. I took it all to the table in the living area. Sol became ecstatic when she saw the wine bottle.

"Oh! Wine! Yummy!"she said, clapping her tiny hands and coming closer.

Romina got out of bed and came over to the table. I knew she was also happy to have some wine, but unlike Sol's joyful excitement, her own reaction was more like that of a starving zombie. I kept trying to make eye contact with her, but she wouldn't look up from her phone. I poured all four glasses. Naty came out of the toilet to join us. She was so pale, she looked green. Glow-in-the-dark green.

"Are you feeling better?" I asked her.

"Yeah, the diarrhea's stopped a little. I don't think there's anything left in my stomach anyways," she answered in a low voice. Her tone was almost sweet and tender.

"It's only water now," Sol added.

"It was water a while ago. Now, it's just nothing," said Naty, back to her angry, bitchy, constipated voice. She sounded tired, nearly defeated.

"Well, but..." Sol tried to apologize.

"No, no. No fighting, girls," I interrupted, raising two glasses. "Here, Naty. I poured some for you too. Take the glasses, ladies! Let's toast!"

"I don't know if I should drink wine," Naty said, although she seemed tempted, her eyes filling once more with life and desire.

"Oh, come on! A little wine never hurt anyone," I told her. "In fact, it will relax you, and that will help you heal," I added.

At first, there was silence. Then some silly comments. Then some giggles. Half a bottle in and we all became long-time best friends, talking about boyfriends, ex-boyfriends, anecdotes, dreams, and wishes. I suggested going out somewhere to have some fun. Naty, fully sweetened by the wine, said her cousin had told her about a party. I wondered who her cousin was. Romina was happy to be included in her social plans. Sol thought it was going to be "super fun." We started to get changed and ready to go. Then we became sisters, dressing, sharing tips, asking each other what to wear, borrowing the hair dryer, all painting our lips red following Sol's technique like we were watching a live Youtube tutorial. A few hours later, we were ready. Naty, whose stomach had started hurting again, locked herself in the toilet so she wouldn't feel like shitting on the street. While we waited, Sol confessed to us that she was bringing along a spare pair of panties for Naty, just in case. She showed us. They were in a ziploc bag inside her purse.

Before walking out the door, I asked Romina if she had spoken to Sebastián. She told me she hadn't since the afternoon.

"Send him a message. Let's see what he's doing tonight." I expected some resistance, but she took out her phone and started typing fast, biting the tip of her tongue.

We went out to the street and waited for a taxi. It was a long time before one showed up. We got in. A woman was driving. A big woman with short hair.

"Where are we girls going tonight?" she asked.

We gave her the party address and she took off, peeling out. She was going so fast that the streetlights on the boulevard seemed to merge into a single continuous line of light. I kept staring, forcing my eyes to stand still, so the line would be straight, a perfect straight bright-orange line. I felt like my brain was printing an fiery electrocardiogram until the woman taxi driver suddenly slammed on the brakes at a traffic light and the line became a wild snake curling on itself, an indecipherable scribble of knots like a massive heart attack. A car had cut her off and she went nuts.

"Men, men, men. They think they know how to do everything. Look at this one, for instance. Then they say that women don't know how to drive. But fuck yeah we know. We know how to drive and cook and do a thousand things more and way better than they do. Don't get me wrong. I love men, but just look at them. They're useless. This one can't even go straight. But we can't live without them, can we girls?" she said.

We girls were speechless.

The party was way out in the middle of nowhere. Before we got out, the taxi driver gave us her card so we *girls* could call her when we *girls* felt like going back. She told us that it was very dangerous to walk around that area, especially if we were alone, especially if we were females. I thought it was weird how she didn't use the word *girls* that time. Romina saved the number in her cell phone, and we said goodbye. Females. That word kept bouncing in my mind until it lost all meaning, just a word, just letters.

Naty seemed to have been overcome by an external force that was controlling her moves. She approached the bouncers at the door as if she owned the place, like she was the one throwing the party. She told them our names. After checking the list, they admitted us. Once inside, she became possessed. She grabbed our arms and ushered us from one place to another. She told us who was who, what they did, who they dated, who they fancied, and how much money they had. She would not stop moving, dragging us around with her. Everyone else was sitting or standing with a drink in their hand. They all looked pretty bored actually, without any interest in whatever the person standing in front of them was talking about. They were all looking out of the corner of their eyes at what else was going on around them. It was curious to see how no one was interested in where they were but rather what was happening wherever they wanted to be. Yet, they stayed put. Although she was moving, Naty was the same. She was talking to us while she walked, but she spent the whole time scanning the room for her cousin. When she finally spotted him, she was startled. He was kissing a blonde bombshell. At first, she turned all red.

Then she took a few quick steps forward but stopped, as if recalculating, and just said, into the air, starting off, "That's not even an actress. Not even a model! I don't even know who she is."

I was as confused as she was, although not about the unknown non-model, non-actress blonde. What confused me was that her cousin was Juan, the guy from the other day at lunch.

"Hey, wait," I said to Romina. "I don't understand. Is he her cousin or is she hooking up with him?"

"No, he's her cousin. I know, it's weird, but that's what she always says anyway."

"Hmm. Sure? He looks like something else. Or someone she'd like to be something else," I told her.

"He's really her cousin. It just annoys her that he doesn't give fuck about her. He doesn't introduce her to people or treat her like the queen she believes herself to be," she said, shrugging her shoulders.

Romina and I couldn't turn away. Naty was going through a metamorphosis, her body contorting, her face twisting. In a flash, she shot towards them, like a runner hearing the starting gun. Sol managed to shout "Naty, nooo!" and tried to grab her, but she slipped away and got between the cousin and the date. The blonde looked down at her—she was over six feet tall without heels—and her cousin, who didn't introduce her, gave her a pat on the back and handed her some drink tickets. Naty stood there gaping, tickets in hand, as the two of them went to the VIP area, which she didn't have access to. I thought she was going to go crazy and jump over the red rope that separated one place from the other. But no. She stayed still. Sol approached quickly, and we walked behind her.

"I feel like going to the toilet. I think I don't feel well," Naty said in a low voice.

"I'll go with you," Sol said, embracing her.

They hugged for a while. I couldn't take my eyes off the free drink tickets held loosely in Naty's hands. I inched forward and took them without any difficulty. Still holding each other, Sol and Naty walked through the crowd and toward the restrooms. Romina and I went the opposite direction, to the bar. We ordered a round of gin and tonics. The bartender put on a phenomenal display. First he set the glasses in a line and majestically tossed in some ice. After jiggling the bottle up and down in front of him and behind his back he poured the gin down the row and opened some cans of tonic with what seemed to be an extra pair of hands, but there was no one else there but him.

"He's an octopus bartender," Romina told me, and we laughed. I tried to grab the drink many times, thinking the process was finished, but there was always another step missing, a little green leaf, a curl of lemon, some herbs to sprinkle, straws cut to perfectly fit the size of the glass.

"Sebastián says he's going to this karaoke place with his friends," Romina told me.

"Ah, I love it!" I cheered. "Shall we?"

"I mean, yeah. This is boring as fuck, but I don't know if the girls are going to want to join us."

"Girls...or females?" I asked.

We both laughed, but Romina abruptly stopped, looked at me confused, and asked, "Wait, what?"

I wanted to explain to her about the woman taxi driver and the girl/female stuff, but my mind kept rewinding further and further away, back in time. To explain completely and in an understandable way felt like too much work. I babbled a few unconnected words before staring at her in silence. She stared back, until we both burst, spitting fancy gin and tonic.

"But, yeah. Naty might be afraid to shit herself," I finally said, feeling a little evil.

"Ha ha! Don't be *such* a bitch," Romina laughed. "Though she actually might."

"Hey, look out, here they both come," I said, pointing.

We managed to convince them again, easily. They put up zero resistance to the idea of the karaoke place. Naty chugged down her gin and tonic even though Sol insisted it might not be good for her "delicate situation."

We left the party together, and once outside we called the woman girl/female taxi driver. While we were waiting, Naty started to feel cramps again. They wouldn't let her back in the party to use the toilet, and her cousin wasn't answering her calls or texts, so she went behind some bushes. When she came back, she said that she had heard strange noises.

"Oh! A female alone!" I shouted.

Romina and I laughed. Then, Romina told her that maybe the noises had just been her belly haunting her. We laughed again, and this time Sol joined in. Naty didn't like it, but she didn't say anything, probably because she was so weakened by her behind-the-bushes experience. Even if nobody had said anything, we would stop laughing for a second, then burst out again, resuming our explosive laughs for no apparent reason, just like that, over and over again. Even Naty started, first with some muffled chuckles and then cackling. When the woman girl/female taxi arrived, honking non stop and switching the lights on and off, the four of us were laughing our asses off, barely able to stand up.

The taxi woman didn't like the idea of us going to karaoke. She didn't think it was a place for girls like us. She tried to convince us to check out some jazz place she usually went to, but we weren't at all interested. "Karaoke sounds more like girls' stuff and jazz sounds more like female stuff," I thought, but I wasn't able to put the idea into words. She drove by the jazz club on the way to the karaoke bar and honked at the door guy to ask how the night was going. I felt sorry for her, because instead of confirming that we had made the wrong decision, he told her that it was a slow night, that we should go to the karaoke down the street.

"It's bumpin' over there," he said.

The taxi woman left us at the door, but it took us a while to get in. Approximately sixty feet of garden separated the sidewalk from the entrance. In the middle of the garden was an artificial lake, and to get to the venue we had to cross a wooden, medieval-looking bridge lined with burning torches. Real fire. I found the scenario not only bizarre, but too hard to process, too much to comprehend, and I burst into loud spitting laughter. Romina got impatient and I had to explain to her.

"I can't, Romina," I told her as seriously as I could. "I just can't. Look, from the end of the bridge to the door isn't far at all, but I don't think I'll be able to control the laughter that walking through the torches will provoke in me."

I pointed out the obstacles. Romina stared at the bridge for a few seconds then started laughing too.

"I'm not going to be able to stop laughing when we get to the door, you know? The end of the bridge and the door are too close. It won't give me enough time to calm down." I was afraid we were going to laugh in the bouncer's face and he wasn't going to let us in.

Sol and Naty were standing between us, looking at me and Romina laughing. Naty tried to hurry us up.

"Don't be stupid! Come on! I really need to go to the toilet again!"

But that made it worse. I had to sit on the curb. I couldn't stop. I couldn't stand. My legs couldn't hold me anymore. They were shaking and felt like candy sticks. Romina sat by my side. We looked like we were in a laughing contest. Her laugh made me laugh more and my laugh made her laugh more. It was a vicious cycle. Sol came closer to us. She tried to make us stop, but she ended up entangled as well. At first she resisted, trying hard not to laugh, but then she started making strange noises. She didn't just snort like a pig; she made the sounds of a whole farm.

"You... you... swallow... swallow... you swallowed Noah's ark!" Romina said.

The three of us were crying, our bodies contorting on the street.

"Hey, fucking motherfuckers! I'm shitting myself, *pendejas!*" Naty shouted.

"Okay, okay," the three of us said. We got up as we promised not to look at each other, pinky swearing then making crosses with them over our lips and kissing them.

We went one by one, single file, separated by increments about three feet. I crossed the bridge with my eyes closed. I felt a warm bubbling in my guts. At the door, we had to pay a hundred-peso cover, which included a drink and *all you can eat* pizza. After that was successfully completed, in order to enter the venue itself, we had to pass through a hallway dimly illuminated by dark blue lights. It was a beautiful tunnel to go through. It looked like outer space. Or the depths of the ocean. I couldn't decide. It was both at the same time. I was ecstatic and tried to take photos with my phone so as to never ever forget that moment but they didn't fully portray what I was actually experiencing, so I just stayed in the middle of the hallway, looking up with my arms into the air until Romina pushed me forward. We emerged from the tunnel and the place was huge, like a hangar, but instead of private jets, it was full of plastic tables, black metal chairs, and people talking loudly. The lights overhead cast a violet hue over everything except one of the walls, which was illuminated with moving red lights. It seemed like the wall was sweating lava. It made me feel very hot and dizzy. I didn't know which way to go. Romina and I looked at each other with disoriented faces, and we hugged each other tight, laughing and crying at the same time until Sebastián showed up. He said he had seen us come in and came over to get us because we seemed lost. He greeted us all with a kiss. He had saved places at his table and led Sol over with his hands on her shoulders. It was impossible to tell Sebastián's friends apart. They were all dressed like twins, or octuplets rather, eight identical human beings with plaid shirts, jeans, and sneakers. They all had the same haircut and the same neat stubble, as if the last time they had all shaved had been on the same day. I wondered if they had planned it or if they were programmed that way. None of them wore a cap. We first ordered our free drink, which turned out to just be a beer, and when it was finished we wanted real drinks. I was tempted by a Lemon Champ. Romina ordered a Bailey's Frozen. Those were the highlights of the menu. Sol and Naty preferred to accept the champagne Sebastián and his friends were drinking, which was free since they were paying, served in fluorescent plastic flutes that looked like they were from a doll set.

The karaoke had a stage with a standing microphone and a giant projection screen at the back. At one point, the lights went out and Catra came out. Everyone was applauding and cheering. Catra was a sort of Marcelo Tinelli[9] of karaoke in Mar del Plata. He was wearing a black suit, white shirt, a bow tie, super tidy and neat. Shiny even.

He waved to everyone and said, "Ladies and gentlemen, welcome" through his wireless microphone. His voice sounded sexy, but a kind of sexy you wouldn't fuck. Ever. Not even if you hadn't fucked for ages. Although he was kind of hot.

Some waitresses in black shorts and white tops handed out cards where everyone could write down their name, table number, and their chosen song for the night's competition. The same waitresses handed out pizza with a little tomato sauce, a little cheese, and some scattered sliced olives. We couldn't stop eating it. Pizza can be really good or really bad, but it's always pizza, and pizza is pizza. Sebastian filled out the card for Sol. He continued to call her Romina, and, instead of explaining the confusion over name, she simply told him that she preferred to be called Sol, her

---

9. Marcelo Tinelli is an Argentine showman known from hosting many horrible TV shows, principally a version of *Dancing with the Stars* in which there are no stars but a lot of not-really-famous people fighting and gossiping onscreen. They also dance. And the whole country watches.

middle name. Naty filled hers out on her own. Romina wrote down Sebastián's friends' names so they would be called up to sing songs by Britney Spears and Cristina Aguilera. Every person from every table, most of them completely drunk, got their turn onstage. When the singing—or whatever it was—was over, there were votes from the public, votes from Catra, votes from the waitresses, and votes from the DJ. We didn't know what the hell he was actually good for, except for pressing the play button. When it was time to announce the winner, the entire room fell silent. Before the waitresses could take our empty glasses, Romina put her straw in her purse. They came with little accordion paper fruits stuck on them, and she wanted them for souvenirs so she could use them to decorate drinks back home. I thought it was disgusting, but also fun, so I let her have mine.

When Catra announced the winners, the sound of pre-recorded trumpets playing in the background (another of the DJ's tasks), the result was not what anyone had expected because Naty had not sung that well nor had she been funny. Nobody even remembered that she had gone on stage. Everyone applauded nonetheless, including our table. Catra encouraged us, and it was impossible to resist his effusive charm. The stage lights shone on Naty. She was beyond ecstatic. She loved the recognition, but mostly she loved the silver plastic tiara being placed on her head by one of the waitresses. She looked at the audience with fascination and even dared to wave with her right hand, moving it side to side like a member of the British royal family. She did have a certain Lady Di air. I realized that Karina and Sofia, my friends that looked like her and worked in supply, also had a Lady Di air, and I got lost a bit in that thought, but not for too long since the whole bar was cheering loudly for Naty. Her eyes looked like they were going to pop out of their sockets again, but, for the first time since I'd met her, from happiness. Her smile was too big to fit on her face. She seemed more like she was at an international awards ceremony for some film she had directed than at a karaoke bar on the Atlantic coast of Buenos Aires.

At the table, Sol feigned enthusiasm despite having lost. She kept clapping, looking side to side, making sure the rest of the audience showed a similar respect and admiration for her beloved winning friend. Catra appeared on the stage once more, microphone in hand. Without looking at him, Naty reached out her hand to take the microphone. He dodged her with style. It seemed he was accustomed to it. The music, just the melody of the Ricky Martin song with which Naty had won, faded and became almost imperceptible.

Then, Catra spoke,

"Guys, I'm afraid there has been a mistake, and it's totally my fault. I'm going to show you, here's the paper with the names. I was wrong, I read the second place as the first."

Naty continued waving like Lady Di, looking at him out of the corner of her eye while he continued talking.

"The winner is Sol Méndez, with the song '*Dejaría todo*' by Chayanne," Catra stated.

People looked at each other, confused. Sol, still in the middle of her standing ovation, didn't seem to react until Sebastián stood, hugged her, and led her to the stage, the place where Naty's smile was slowly disappearing and slight traces of terror were starting to show on her face, like vines growing over a recently whitewashed wall.

It must have only taken seconds for Catra to remove the tiara from Naty's head and crown Sol, who was petrified. For me, it felt like an eternity, long minutes in which I couldn't take my eyes off Naty's face. I was able to record everything moment by moment, frame by frame, as if my vision was a professional Hollywood movie camera that was filming in slow motion. Her expression of victory and happiness turned to surprise, confusion, helplessness, then finally reached a sorrow that moved my heart, even.

I raised my glass of Lemon Champ in the air and yelled at Romina, "She won the Oscar for best film!"

Romina, who was just taking a sip from her glass, instantly spit out a mouthful of Bailey's Frozen with such force that she sent her straw with the paper accordion cherry on the tip flying. Because she was trying to catch the straw she wanted so much to protect, Romina missed Naty's outburst. Like the loser in a beauty pageant, she snatched Sol's tiara from her head, nimbly evaded Sebastián's failed attempts to catch her, and crossed the entire room, running as fast as she could toward the exit.

The crowd was bewildered. Everything was silent except for Chayanne's faint melody in the background. The first to run after Naty was Romina, still clutching the straw with the paper cherry, and I followed.

We found Naty standing in the middle of the street, holding the tiara, squeezing it with both hands.

When she saw us, she got scared and shouted, "It's mine! They gave it to me first! It's mine! You can't take it away from me!"

"Naty, don't be stupid. It's only karaoke," Romina told her, pointing at her with the straw, the cherry half collapsed, all wet and sticky.

"No! Shut up! It's mine!" she shouted, and she started to walk backwards.

I don't know if the rest of the karaoke people, who by that time were mostly outside watching the scene, saw it coming. A cyclist came careening down the street, dressed all in black—leggings, a tight t-shirt and a cap, a wide cap— at times illuminated by the street lights then disappearing in total darkness. He reminded me of the Thrush that night I had run into him. He looked like a black horse gliding down the sidewalk. I followed him with my eyes, imagining he was galloping through a meadow until Naty entered my field of vision and my brain automatically projected the bicycle's trajectory. Naty was right in his way. Despite the fact that he yelled "Watch out!" she didn't react or move. He tried to dodge her, and she lost her balance, walking backwards, stumbling, probably trying to find equilibrium again but losing it more and more, her knees bending, her legs acting autonomously, having lost all communication with her brain, twisting in weird, desperate ways. She stumbled to a construction zone marked off with cones and yellow tape that were set up to block a hole in the street and signal danger. But nothing could stop her. She grabbed at the tape, but of course it didn't hold, and, just like that, she disappeared into the open hole behind her. A sewer. A hole full of shit.

The firefighters arrived first and began an operation to extract Naty from the shit hole. Naty's screams echoed off the sewer walls. They had a difficult time calming her down, and she wasn't responding to their instructions. The bicyclist was lying on the ground. No one had wanted to touch him, not even the firefighters.

"We have to wait for the paramedics. The ambulance should be here any minute" they said.

Romina and I approached him. He looked familiar.

"He's the Mexican from the movie," I told Romina, almost whispering, as if I wasn't sure it was him, even though it definitely was.

"What Mexican?" she asked me, confused, chewing the tip of the straw with half the cherry.

"The one from the cinema. The one with the open fly! The director!" I reminded her, screaming excitedly.

"You're right!" Romina was amazed.

From the tight black leggings he was wearing, I realized he very well might have been wearing boxers that day at the movies, because you could tell he was pretty well-endowed. Also, he had his cap, but I couldn't remember if it was the same one he'd been wearing before.

"I don't understand why they wear caps at night," Romina said.

"Oh, because it's original, so they take it everywhere, you

know? Look at the sticker," I told her, remembering Naty's explanation. Then, turning to him, I asked, "Hey, Mexican! Are you okay?"

He didn't answer us but made a sign with his hand. We didn't really know what it meant, but it seemed to be some sort of *OK* signal and we relaxed. But then we saw there was blood pooling around his head and we got scared.

"Don't move, the ambulance will arrive any second," we told him.

The firefighters were still trying to calm Naty when the paramedics arrived. They attended to the Mexican first. Naty was still in the shit hole anyway. They used scissors to cut off his original cap (with a sticker) so they could check his head. It was painful to watch. It turned out he only had a scratch, there was no open wound whatsoever. The paramedics explained to us that it was normal for there to be so much blood. The human scalp bleeds a lot, even from superficial abrasions. It was an interesting fact I would never forget. They also asked him some questions to test his reactions. He knew it was November 20, 2017, that his name was Luis Ángeles Martínez, that he was in Mar del Plata, Buenos Aires, Argentina and that he was 46 years old. He correctly counted four, seven, and eight of the paramedic's fingers and followed the flashlight's light with his eyes. They asked him if he had medical insurance and Luis Ángeles Martínez told them that he had traveler's insurance with his credit card. However, it was determined that the traveler's insurance didn't cover the costs of doing a CT scan to rule out concussion or brain damage, so they asked him if he had fainted or lost consciousness at any point. Luis Ángeles assured them he had not. Then the paramedics told him to stay calm. He didn't need to be afraid of sleeping as usual tonight, but if he felt anything weird or experienced dizziness or any sort of confusion, he should go to the emergency room.

When the firefighters were finally able to pull Naty out of the sewer, she was covered in shit. It wasn't thick shit. It was more like dissolved shit, a brown liquid with some more concentrated parts that covered everything: her feets, legs, abdomen, chest, face, head, even the plastic tiara. The paramedics tried to get closer to her, but they had a hard time. She was having a mental breakdown and was screaming.

"I'm cursed! I'll always be full of shit! I'm cursed!" she kept repeating, over and over, nonstop.

"Calm down, ma'am. Calm down and let us help you,"the firefighters or paramedics would tell her, trying to get closer.

But Naty kept screaming. Her eyes, the only part of her not covered in shit, were wide.

Sol couldn't stop crying. She was heartbroken, saying it was her fault for leaving Naty alone that day she crossed paths with the fortune tellers. Sebastián hugged her and tried to comfort her, calling her Romina.

"Remember that I like to be called Sol, my middle name," she told him as she snuggled into his chest.

Romina and I approached Naty in an attempt to calm her down. She let us get closer. An aura of nauseating stench surrounded her. The smell was so disgusting, so unbearable, that I found it impossible to stop gagging. She kept repeating that she was cursed, and we told her that the curse was already fulfilled because she had already fallen into shit, and it was not going to happen to her again. But despite our logical reasoning, she shook her head, faster and faster. It was like a shampoo commercial, but instead of radiating freshness she was splashing shit all around her. She wanted to go look for the *gitana*. When she tried to run, the paramedics, with the help of the firefighters, intercepted her, took her to the ambulance and strapped her down to the stretcher because she wouldn't stop moving, kicking her legs and waving her arms. She was given intravenous sedatives. They kicked in fast. Then the paramedics were able to look her over. She wasn't seriously injured. They found only some scratches under her outer layer of shit, which they were wiping away with clean cloths. We asked if we could accompany her to the hospital. They told us only family members were allowed. I wanted to explain that she was alone in the city and we were her friends, but Romina spoke first. She said we were second cousins, from different marriages of Naty's father's brother. I was surprised they let us into the ambulance, no ID or proof required. They were probably used to seeing and hearing so many wild things that the explanation of Romina's family ties seemed normal. Sol was still crying. Sebastián told us he would take care of her, that she was in no emotional state to go with us. We left her with him and asked him to grab our stuff, which we had left in the karaoke bar. From the rear window of the ambulance, we could see them walking back to the club, their arms around each other as they crossed the bridge with the torches.

Even after they had cleaned Naty, the smell inside the ambulance was still nauseating. Naty was babbling incomprehensibly. The driver accelerated quickly, and the sirens were on. He ran the red lights and took the corners fast. During one of the turns, Romina threw up. The smell of vomit mixed with the smell of shit was too much for me to handle and made my stomach turn. The paramedic who was riding in the back with us realized that I was also about to throw up. He tried to hand me a bag but he didn't make it in time and my vomit flew through the air, like a scene from a movie about outer space.

The ambulance took us directly to the emergency ward. "Well, isn't this VIP treatment?" I thought, but I couldn't say it because when I opened my mouth I felt like throwing up again. They took Naty out on the stretcher, still restrained. She disappeared down the hallway, pushed by running hospital staff and paramedics. They brought us wheelchairs. Even when we assured them we could walk, they insisted, saying it was hospital procedure. They left us alone for a while in the ER waiting room, so white, illuminated with fluorescent lights that hurt our eyes. There was a television in one of the corners that displayed patients' names and the number of the examination room they were called to. We were the only ones in the waiting room. None of the first names were the same, but the surnames were all variations on the same two. The two guys who had those last names must have had a great time back in the day. The doors that led deeper into the hospital were closed, but the one leading outside was slightly ajar, and a cold breeze was coming in. Outside, everything was black and dark. It gave me the feeling of being on a military base in Antarctica. Romina did not agree with me. She said that if it were Antarctica it would be much colder and we would be wearing orange thermal suits. I wanted to prove her wrong, but she was right so I shut up and we remained silent.

Two nurses suddenly showed up. They pushed us in our wheelchairs to another room where a third nurse sat in front of a desktop PC. It seemed shiny and brand new, but it looked like an antique. It had a square monitor and a clunky keyboard. The massive computer dominated the entire desk, infinite cables coming in and out with twinkling red and green lights in their input, or outputs. I couldn't tell, even when I tried to follow the cables with my eyes. They weren't tangled, but there were so many that I got dizzy and lost and went cross-eyed. I had to shake my head and focus on something else, but between posters with information about dengue, yellow fever, STDs, drug abuse, mental health, and adoption-not-abortion as well as cabinets with medical instruments, nothing was soothing. The two nurses who had pushed us took out a little white gun with a green light, which they placed on our foreheads to take our temperatures. One after the other, they read the results out loud, and the third put them into the computer. She typed fast. The keyboard sounded like a melody, and the nurses voices were a choir. Their movements and words were completely synchronized. A perfect performance. A scene from a musical. The nurses put a little clip, also white, on our pointer fingers, one for each of us. Once again, they read out our pulses. I expected them to break out in a dance at any point, and I got anxious. But they just took our blood pressure with those inflatable arm bands that hurt without hurting, and the devices beeped because our pressure was too low. The nurses looked at each other, then simultaneously turned their gaze on us.

"Are either of you allergic to any medication?" they asked in unison.

We both answered no. Me, low and doubting. Romina, high and defensive.

"We are going to give you something to hydrate you and a little glucose for your blood pressure," they informed us as they pushed us in our wheelchairs to another hallway.

They delivered us to yet another nurse, who took the papers from the other nurses without looking up. She didn't raise her head, but instead just kept her gaze on what was in front of her, anything but us. I wondered if her head was just like that, permanently fallen, the neck unable to support it. She never met our eyes, not even when she made us stretch out our right arms or when she pressed our veins with a rubber band or gave us a cotton swab with alcohol or inserted our IVs. I moved my head, rotating it, as if I was stretching or doing a yoga exercise, trying to insert myself in her field of vision. My neck bones cracked loudly. It actually felt nice, and for a second I forgot what I was doing or where I was until she attached the bottle thing containing something to hydrate us and the glucose stuff for our blood pressure.

Finally, she looked at me and asked "Is your neck okay?"

I was startled but mostly embarrassed.

I said, "Yes," and looked down. I was dying to ask about her neck, but not only did it feel inappropriate, but I could see now that it actually worked fine. The bottle things held over a liter each, and the nurse hung them together on a hook on top of a high pole. She checked to make sure the drip was flowing and left.

I wanted to cry. I'd never liked needles, and this one was hurting my arm. No matter the position I tried, I felt it sadistically piercing my flesh, whatever liquid it carried entering and invading my veins. But I held on. There was nothing I could do about it, and if there had been I would have been too tired anyway. The hospital hallway no longer looked like a military base in Antarctica. It was light blue, with a gray ceramic floor, sort of like the hallway of an old public school. The chairs that lined it were either black or red, arranged in no specific pattern. There were two more people on IV's just like us. One was in a wheelchair, hugging his belly. He seemed like he was asleep, but at times he would open his eyes and scream in pain. There was also a toothless homeless man, covered in patches of dirt. He walked up and down the hallway, carrying his IV pole in one hand and a plastic grocery bag in the other. He was barefoot and greeted every hospital worker he saw including security guards and cleaning staff, using their full names. Each returned the greeting, using his name, cheerfully sweet. There were other people waiting, mostly dozing off in the chairs, as well as a lady laying on a stretcher that had been pushed against a wall so as not to block the walkway. It was the VIP departure lounge of horror.

"Where the fuck is Naty?" Romina asked.

"Her flight already left," I answered, almost without thinking.

"What?" she said, looking at me strangely.

"Nothing, nothing, I don't know," I told her, trying to think clearly.

"We should go ask," Romina said. She was serious now.

"Yes, we should. But first let's ask them to take these things out of us. They're almost empty," I said, pointing to the little remaining liquid.

"Mine is done, and my tube is filled with blood." She looked disgusted.

We got up and dragged the pole between us to the nurses' room. They made us wait while they were putting IVs into other patients. Our tubes became increasingly filled with blood. Sure that I would faint, I tried to avoid looking. Seeing my own blood outside of my body, either coming out on its own or being extracted, made me feel like I was being sucked dry, slowly emptied. A part of me was now on the outside, where it could be handled by strangers. What if they took something vital? It was terrifying. It felt like when you send nudes to someone who you later break up with and you know the pictures are now out there in the world. One of the nurses finally came over and released us from everything we were plugged into. I'd never felt so relieved in my life. While she was taping a cotton ball over the needle hole, we asked if she knew anything about the girl that had come with us in the ambulance.

"The open sewer one?" she asked. I thought about how later, when she would tell the story to her friends, she would refer to Naty as the patient who had been brought in covered in shit. I kind of giggled, but I managed to choke it back with a cough.

"Yes, that one," Romina told her, keeping her tone serious and giving me an icy-mommy side look to make me behave appropriately.

"She's being examined," the nurse answered. "Are you related?" Her voice was firm.

"Second cousins, from different marriages of her father's brother," Romina lied again.

"Wait out there," she told us, grimacing in obvious suspicion. Or maybe she was forcing solemnity to hold back her own laughter.

We waited for over an hour in the departure VIP horror lounge, but no one came. We asked the nurse again, and she told us that we had to keep waiting. Naty was undergoing tests.

"I'm tired of being in here. I'm getting depressed," I told Romina.

"Me too. Besides, I'm fucking starving," she answered.

"Well, maybe we could go out and eat something, and then we'll come back," I proposed, standing up.

We went to the nurses' room and spoke to the same nurse. She was filling out some papers at a desk. Romina asked her if there was a place to eat nearby.

"There's nothing close. You'll either have to eat in the hospital cafeteria or order delivery," she answered, looking over the top of her glasses.

"What kind of delivery is there?" Romina asked.

The nurse opened a drawer and took out a pile of food delivery flyers.

"There's everything: sushi, Chinese, regional, salads, vegetarian, vegan, rolls. But at this hour, only the guys from the pizza place will come."

She looked through the flyers like she was flipping through a deck of cards until she found the one from the pizza place and handed it to us.

"Please bring it back to me when you're done, okay?"

We asked her for the address, but she told us, "Just tell them you're at the hospital."

We read the menu and reviewed our options. I wanted two spicy meat empanadas.

"The meat-cut-with-a-knife ones, not the ground-beef ones," I told Romina.

She wanted one *humita*[10] empanada and a ham-and-cheese one. We also decided on a big mozzarella-and-garlic pizza and a large Coke. What we really wanted was beer, but it was overpriced. We were salivating with desire, but just as we were about to call the pizza place, we realized that we had left all our things, including our wallets and phones, at the karaoke bar. We checked our pockets. In my jeans there were thirty-four pesos stuck to pieces of a receipt from the Chinese grocery store on the corner by my house, which I

---

10. *Humita* is a filling of corn paste or crushed corn kernels, to which is added a fried dish generally prepared with onion, tomato and ground red chili pepper.

had forgotten to take out before doing a load of laundry. They were twisted into a solid mass. Romina had twenty-seven pesos in coins and the woman taxi driver's business card. Neither of us had our phones. We had to go back to the nurse, who assumed we were just returning the pamphlet, and ask to use the phone. She ended up placing the order for us. We had to sacrifice the pizza and the Coke because we couldn't afford it. We only got the empanadas. It was such a sad moment.

The order arrived quite quickly. We had to go to the hospital main door to meet the delivery guy. Romina thought it was best to eat outside and get some fresh air. I agreed. Even though it was chilly, it was way better than being inside the hospital and that way I could also smoke a cigarette after we finished. I sat to one side of the stairs that led up to the door, and Romina went to get two glasses of water from the dispenser in the hall. It was almost dawn. The nurse was right. There was nothing nearby. No houses, no cars, no places to eat. Nothing. Just trees, grass, and sky. It seemed like we were in the middle of the country.

"Is the meat one delicious?" Romina asked, looking at my empanada.

"It's super good, very spicy. Knife-cut style is the best. Ground beef is so bad. Do you want a bite?"

"No, thank you, I can't handle spicy," she answered.

"Imagine if Naty ate it. Fireworks would come out her ass," I said, laughing.

"Hahaha, shut up!" she said, trying to keep from cracking up.

"Sorry. It was such an easy joke. You handed it to me on a silver platter," I said. "But seriously, do you think she'll stop shitting some day?" I really wondered if her diarrhea would last forever.

"You know, I don't understand why she didn't just buy an activated charcoal tablet and be done with the whole thing. It would have been like putting a plug in her butt, and she would have been finished with all that shit. It's like she purposely chose to shit in every fucking toilet. Even in the street. Even herself," Romina said.

"I know, right? Finished with all that shit," I said and I started laughing again while she took another bite of the empanada.

"Hahahaha, how can you be so stupid?" Romina responded, wiping her hands with a paper napkin that wouldn't soak up any of the grease that covered our empanadas.

"She probably didn't want to pay for it. The charcoal thing," I thought out loud.

"Oh. That's definitely it."

When we finished eating, I lit a cigarette and Romina asked me for a few puffs. Instead, I gave her a whole cigarette. It really bothered me not to be able to smoke my own in peace.

"But I'm not going to smoke it all," she told me.

"Well, throw it away, or put it out when you've had enough and save it for next time you want to ask me for another puff," I answered, a little irritated.

"Ay! Don't be a crazy bitch with me."

"Sorry. It's just that it's almost six in the morning," I told her.

"Already? Fuck. Hey, Sol really erased herself from this picture, didn't she?" she said, looking at her watch.

"She has probably been fucking Sebastián all night," I guessed.

"For sure. *Call me Sol! Call me by my middle name!*" Romina said, imitating Sol's voice.

We both laughed hard, but we were tired. We just opened our mouths and made extreme laughing body movements, but hardly any noise came out.

Romina put out her half-smoked cigarette and said, "I mean, she said she felt guilty about leaving Naty alone that morning with the *gitanas*, but now she's left her again. Her BFF."

When I finished smoking, we put the trash in the same

bag the empanadas had come in and threw it in a bin in the hall. We went back to where the nurse was. When she saw us, she waved us over. A woman came out of a door. She was tall but looked even taller because she was wearing high heels. She was also wearing glasses with metal frames, tight black pants and a green shirt, and a white apron. I was stunned by how shiny her hair was.

"Are you Natalia López's cousins?" she asked, pointing at us with a fancy black-and-gold pen.

"Yes," we answered simultaneously

"I'm Dr. María Negrín, the on-call psychiatrist. Natalia's fall only caused scratches and bruises. She presents signs of dehydration and..."

"Because of her diarrhea," I interrupted, thinking out loud.

"She's been sick for several days," Romina added.

"We didn't think it was that serious," I reflected, feeling a little guilty for having laughed so hard at the situation.

The doctor looked at us like we were stupid and ignorant. We felt her stare and remained silent.

"Natalia is in a very delicate state," she said very seriously. "We had to sedate her. She speaks inconsistently about fortune tellers and curses. She believes she is possessed. Although she did not express suicidal intent, we believe that she might be a risk to herself or others." Her voice was low, her tone soft but firm. She wanted to make sure we clearly understood what she was saying.

Neither Romina nor I said anything. We stood there and stared into the doctor's eyes, which were also black and shiny, waiting for her to continue her explanation. Fragments of what had happened over the last few days came into my mind. I felt as if the doctor was scolding us for not having helped sooner, for having made fun of Naty. I looked at the floor. Romina did the same. It was only then that we realized this was some actual shit.

"We need to notify a direct family member so they can take responsibility for her, but no one answered any of the numbers she gave us."

"We're her second cousins," Romina said, ever-faithful to the lie.

"It has to be a direct family member," she emphasized. "Otherwise, we have to keep her hospitalized and under observation."

"Until when?" Romina asked.

"Until they come looking for her."

"Can we at least see her?" Romina asked.

We followed Dr. Negrín through hallways, up stairs, and into an elevator. The hospital constantly changed shape, color, lighting, and furniture. Blue, incandescent, plastic; pink, soft, acrylic; green, warm, comfortable. Then we reached the white, cold, and bare.

Naty was inside a room with glass windows facing the hallways and two barred windows facing outdoors. She was lying on the bed. Everything was white. She had either been bathed or meticulously cleaned. She looked purified. She was wearing an extremely white robe and had a tube in her arm. Romina and I looked at each other. We didn't know what to do or say. We could see her lips moving. She was mumbling something, talking to herself. She turned her head and saw us. She stayed still for a few seconds before slowly getting up and walking to the hallway window, dragging the IV. She placed both hands on the glass. Her face looked like someone else's. She stared at us, then let out a high-pitched, tearful scream. We remained silently frozen in place until two nurses came running down the hallway and opened the door. Dr. Negrín followed them. They put her back in bed and fiddled with the tube. They closed the curtains, also white, and we couldn't see anything else.

We couldn't get her out, and they wouldn't give us her things. Neither of us had any of her relatives' phone numbers.

We didn't even know her parents' names. I had only recently learned her last name. Romina believed she was an only child but wasn't sure.

"The best thing to do would be to go back and talk to Sol. She would know," she told me.

"What about her cousin? Her real cousin, or hookup, or whatever. I don't know, that actor guy?" I asked.

"He's her cousin, Carolina. I told you already. They're just weird. Or she's just weird. Anyways, who knows where he is. Let's just make Sol take charge of this. She's supposedly her best friend since kindergarten. We came here, we waited, we did as much as we could."

"I know, but I feel a little sorry for her," I answered.

"They drugged her again. She might not even remember anything about tonight. Besides, I have to go to work tomorrow or they're going to fucking fire me. And I do not want to give them that pleasure," Romina said, her anger rising.

"Wait. How are we going to go back to Buenos Aires without Naty?" I asked.

"The fucking bus. We'll take the fucking bus."

And we left the hospital.

I felt defeated. It was partially because we couldn't do shit about Naty, but mostly because I hate buses. You couldn't open the windows and you couldn't ask them to stop so you could take a smoke break. Although, in that sense, it wasn't so different from riding in Naty's car.

We didn't have money left to take a taxi, so we started walking. The sun was up, but the day was cloudy and cold. The wind blowing in our faces was very annoying, and I hated not having my sunglasses. I wished I had my cap. We walked for hours past open fields. The lower clouds moved one direction and the higher ones went in another. At times they would leave open holes of uncovered sky, blue circles through which the sun's rays shone, projecting bright green circles on the grass and casting halos of milky white light, similar to the ones made by a film projector or a spotlight. Several bright spots would appear at once. Romina ran off the road to get into one.

"What the fuck are you doing?" I yelled, surprised to see her actually running into the middle of nowhere.

"I'm cold! I need the sun's warmth!" she answered as she ran clumsily.

When she reached the bright spot closest to her, she closed her eyes and opened her arms like the statue of Christ the Redeemer. She stood in the center of the circle, enveloped by the sun's rays. It looked like she was going to be teleported away at any moment. I had the sudden feeling I was about to be left alone. Then, I would have to walk back by myself. I ran and stood in another circle, close to hers, eyes closed and arms open. The feeling of warmth was beautiful. But after a few minutes clouds covered the hole. The air grew cold again, and we were still in the middle of nowhere. We continued walking quickly, at the same pace, without speaking. But we never seemed to arrive anywhere. We were still so far away, and we had no idea where the fuck we were. After a long while, suddenly, streets started to take shape, then houses, stores, buildings, traffic lights, corners, cars. People appeared, just starting their days. At some point, Romina slowed her pace and fell behind me. I kept turning my head to check that she was still there so we wouldn't lose each other. Later, she sped up and eventually passed me. Then she was the one looking over her shoulder to make sure I was following her.

When we finally reached the apartment building, my body was exhausted. I was destroyed. My eyes, my legs, my whole body was swollen. I just wanted to go to sleep. But we realized we didn't have the keys. We rang the bell several times, but no one answered us. We could see that the apartment window was open. We tried to put together a plan on how to climb up there. We tossed around some ideas, but it was impossible, even though the apartment was on a low floor. We were considering sleeping on the street when someone came out and we sneaked in. We went up the stairs, sure we would have to kick the door in, but it opened with just a little push.

All the lights were on. Someone was in the bathroom, taking a shower. We assumed it was Sol. Romina started banging on the door, and when Sol answered that she would be out in a minute, she threw herself on the bed. Everything we had left at the karaoke bar was on the table. Sol emerged from the bathroom surrounded by a cloud of vapor, her body and head wrapped in her violet towels.

"Hi! You took your time getting home, didn't you?" She looked totally unbothered, steam rising from her skin.

"We were at the hospital until dawn," Romina answered.

Sol looked at us as if we had just told her we had just come back from buying chewing gum. She took the towel off her head and began to blow dry her hair. Romina and I were waiting for some kind of reaction. Questions, intrigue, drama, anything, but she continued drying her hair like nothing had happened. Romina moved toward her slowly, until she was right in front of her face.

"Sol, Naty is hospitalized, and they won't let her leave unless a family member checks her out. She's having some sort of psychotic crisis."

"And we had to walk back, the whole way back, from the hospital," I added.

Once again, there was complete and utter silence.

"Sol, you have to call Naty's parents," Romina said firmly, trying to unfreeze Sol's thought process and speed things up.

"Me? Why me?" Sol asked. I didn't know if she was playing dumb or actually being dumb. She raised her shoulders and pointed at herself with her comb.

While Romina explained the whole situation over and over again to Sol, who seemed oblivious or simply didn't want to react or just didn't give a fuck, I sat in the chair and put my head between my legs. My blood pressure had dropped. It was then that I saw that the floor was covered with crumpled paper bags. With my eyes, I followed their trail, which led me straight to the refrigerator. All the interior drawers, shelves, and trays had been removed and piled on the kitchen floor. I opened the door and found hundreds of sea lions, little boats, many kinds of Virgin Marys, lighthouses, and an insane variety of more color-changing souvenirs. I wanted to know how many there were, but there were so many I couldn't keep count. When I started again for the third time, Sol's high pitched voice interrupted me.

"What are you doing? Close the door!" she yelled at me, pushing me away from the refrigerator. "If I take them out of the fridge, they turn blue. Look, the ones in the freezer are more violet. I just love them when they're purple."

"I see. And how do you plan to take them back home? Are you taking the fridge with you?" I asked.

"Don't be silly! You're always so silly!" she said, giggling. "Sebastián is going to come pick me up with a cooler. He also told me to remind you not to forget to clean the apartment before you go because if you don't, he won't return the cleaning deposit."

She closed the refrigerator door and turned around to go back to the living room, but Romina stood in front of her.

"You also lived here these past three days. So you have to clean too. Especially this pile of crumpled paper and all Naty's and your dirty dishes."

"I didn't use any dishes. That was Naty. Make her clean them!" she yelled back.

"Naty is fucking hospitalized, Sol! I just explained it to you! You have to contact her parents!" Romina shouted even louder, grabbing Sol by the shoulders.

Sol opened her eyes wide. That was her only reaction. She kind of looked like she was going to cry, but she didn't. She just held that expression for minutes. It was impressive. I had never seen anyone do that. Not for such a long time anyways. I almost complimented her on her skills, but then I remembered about Naty and thought that maybe a less aggressive technique was needed to bring Sol to her senses.

"Sol, do you know any of Naty's relatives? Do you know her mom? Her dad?" I asked, sweet and gentle.

"Hmm...Yes, but Naty doesn't get along with them," she answered, staring at the floor while shuffling her feet like a five-year-old.

"Well, we should call them anyway. If we don't, they'll leave Naty locked up. Do you want Naty to stay locked up in a psychiatric ward? All alone? Your BFF since kindergarten?" I tried to persuade her, still using a soft tone.

"Well, no... No. No no no. But I can't call her parents. I don't have time. I have to get my things ready because Sebastian is coming to pick me up any minute," she said, and she slipped away to the nursery.

My brain got stuck, paralyzed in total confusion. I felt like my face was the same, frozen. My brain didn't know which expression to activate in order to be able to show what I was experiencing: laughter, sadness, indignation, fury, fear. It couldn't decide which one of them best suited the situation. Then it sent them all at once. My face went dark and I laughed, but my brain realized that it was inappropriate and aborted. I let out a small cry. I could feel myself smiling exorbitantly, but I was panicked. Romina was determined in her emotions. I could clearly see her rage. She was about to kill Sol.

"Sol! Naty is hospitalized! Don't you fucking get it?" she yelled.

"Yes, yes, I do get it! But her parents are divorced and Sebastian is coming to pick me up," Sol explained to her simply, calmly.

"Oh, really? Fuck this. You know, I'm tired, and I want to go to sleep, and Naty is your friend, your stupid fucking BFF, so take charge of this situation and call her parents!" Romina answered, imitating Sol's tone.

Romina grabbed Sol's phone and pushed it into her hand. Sol started searching through her contacts, but before she could open one of them, she received a call. It was Sebastián. He was around the corner.

"I don't have time to call anyone. Sorry! I have to change my clothes and get everything ready. Here. Here's the number. You can call them if you want." She gave the phone back to Romina and locked herself in the nursery.

Sol got dressed, put all her stuff in her bag, combed her bangs, and painted her lips red while she sang something. When she finished, she came out of the nursery and sat down at the table. We stared at her.

"What?" she asked. "I'll grab the souvenirs right before I leave so that they don't change temperature. Don't you understand that if I take them out of the refrigerator they'll change color?"

Sebastián arrived and entered without knocking. In one hand, he held an ice cream cone that he wouldn't stop licking. He carried a cooler in his other hand.

"Hi! You brought ice, didn't you?" Sol asked as soon as they were done kissing, they're entangled tongues clearly visible to everyone. It made me want to throw up.

"Yep. Two bags, as requested," he answered, pointing at the cooler.

Sol grabbed it and went to the kitchen, where we could hear her moving the souvenirs from the fridge to the cooler.

"What a night last night, huh?" Sebastián said. We stayed silent. "And what about your friend Naty?"

"She's hospitalized," I told him.

"Poor thing. But I'm sure she'll be okay."

"What about the deposit?" Romina asked.

"Let me know before you leave, and I'll come by to check the apartment and bring it to you. Then you can also give me back the key," Sebastián told us.

"Come on, Sebastián. It's getting late," Sol said as she left the room, "Bye, girls! Talk soon! Have fun!" She waved as she disappeared through the door with all her things. Sebastián followed her.

When the door closed, we spent eternal minutes staring at it in silence until the ideas in our minds started settling and we began to laugh like never before, lying on the floor. We couldn't speak. We could only make laughing noises, which made us laugh even more, until we snorted like pigs.

When we got over it a little, Romina dialed Naty's parents, who didn't pick up. She left several voice messages. She was uncomfortable with just informing an answering machine about what was going on. Anxiously, she started a frenetic scroll through Naty's Facebook.

"I'm an expert at this. This is how I discovered that that idiot Juan Manuel, who wanted to be my official boyfriend all the time, was with someone else. The guy posted a photo of a coffee and a croissant, saying 'A delicious coffee after a delicious night,' or something like that, tagging another girl while we were still fucking dating," she told me quickly, excited.

"You shouldn't check guys' facebook like that, Romina. It's bad for you. If you already know he's an idiot, just tell him to fuck off and be done with it," I told her.

"I know, but I can't help it. It's stronger than I am. It's addictive. Plus, I'm fucking good at it," she answered without taking her eyes off the screen.

After some exhaustive stalking, Romina found Naty's cousin's account and another belonging to someone who seemed to be her aunt. She sent them messages. Only the cousin answered, thinking we were joking at first. Romina insisted until the cousin finally promised to call Naty's mother, although Naty's mother had not spoken to the cousin's mother, Naty's aunt, for a long time. They'd gotten into a big fight over an inheritance or something related to money.

"It turns out they really are cousins, see?" Romina said.

I started to tidy up the apartment. I washed Naty's dishes. I threw away the rotten fruit. Even the apple had gone bad—such a waste of perfection. I put the drawers and trays inside the refrigerator, picked up the papers, swept up the sand and let the water run in the shower to wash away the soap and shampoo foam and stray hairs until they all became a massive ball that I picked up with some toilet paper. Finally, it was time to enter the nursery. The eyes of the lamp statue followed me around the room, and I tried hard to ignore her stare. The room smelled like shit. At first, I thought I was imagining things, but then in the corner I found a grocery bag with all of Naty's dirty clothes inside. That's where the smell was coming from. Gagging, I grabbed the bag and threw it out the window. I realized, too late, when it was already in mid-air, that it might hit someone. I held still for a few moments, waiting for a scream or some cursing. Nothing. I kept going. Everything else that was lying around I put in Naty's suitcase. Once finished, I came out and organized my own things. To prevent my cap from getting smashed, I hooked it to the handle of my suitcase.

"I'm going to sleep a bit. I can't even be alive anymore," I told Romina when I was done.

"I found a bus that leaves at twelve. There were empty seats, so I bought two tickets," Romina said.

"Does it have those bed-type seats? Or just regular seats?" I asked.

"Yeah. Semi-bed it says."

"Semi-bed is not bed. They're semi-seats more than semi-beds," I told her.

"Well, that's the only bus tonight with available seats. So unless you want to stay, that's the one we're taking," she answered, standing up.

"Ok. Whatever. I already cleaned up and put everything away," I answered.

"Naty's things too?" she asked.

"Yeah. Except the bag full of shit-covered clothes. I threw that out the window, like a shit bomb into the street," I told her while I threw myself on the bed.

"What? You could have hit someone!" she said.

"Yeah, yeah. But you know what? I didn't." I told her. I was still mad about the semi-bed bus.

But after a few seconds of tense silence, we started giggling softly. We fell asleep laughing. When I woke up, it was dark. I checked the clock, worried we might have overslept, but we had plenty of time. Romina was still sleeping, and I went to take a shower. As I went in, I saw the imported shampoo and conditioner were still there. I had missed those while I was cleaning. They were hiding in between the shower curtains. I used some of each and wondered if Sol had forgotten them or if they were Naty's. I would never have forgotten them. They were fucking expensive. Sol had forgotten them, certainly. Naty wasn't the type to spend that much money on hair products. Or maybe she was. Those sorts of spending inconsistencies were typical among the habitually stingy. Anyway, they had hardly been used, so when I finished, I dried the bottles with my towel and put them in a bag to take home. I felt so happy, like I had received an unexpected gift. A surprise prize.

When I came out, Romina was still in bed but she was awake. Naty's cousin had answered her message. He'd spoken with Naty's mother, who'd spoken with Naty's father, and the two of them were coming to Mar del Plata, the mother by plane and the father by car because they were divorced and couldn't stand each other. It seemed that everything had ended very badly.

"And what do they plan to do when they check her out of the hospital?" I asked. "Are they each going to take half of her?"

Romina thanked him and told him we were going to leave Naty's bag with Sol, who also knew which parking lot the car was in. While Romina was taking a shower, I told Sebastián we were about to leave. He said he'd come by in a while.

While we waited, we uncorked the remaining bottle of wine. We drank it from the bottle so as not to get any glasses dirty again. Sebastián arrived when we were halfway through the bottle. Sol was with him. While Sebastián checked out the apartment, Sol showed us photos of how she had placed her souvenirs in the kitchen window of Sebastián's apartment, but since there wasn't room for them all, she had put the rest in the bathroom. Romina gave her Naty's bag and told her that her cousin was going to pick it up. We all left together and stood in the doorway looking at each other for a while until Romina told them we had to leave to catch the bus.

The only thing Sol said was, "Have a good trip," and she sent us off with a noisy kiss and left, hand in hand with Sebastián. We stared at her as she walked away.

"The truth is that I admire her a little," I told Romina. "She seemed so silly, but in one day—less than a day—the girl dumped her boyfriend who she was building a house with and settled in this boy's house and decorated it with souvenirs."

"Her boyfriend wasn't that cute or cool either," she responded.

"When do you think she'll tell him her real name is Sol, not Romina?" I asked.

"Never. Unless they get married." She stopped for a second "I mean, they probably will."

We were silent for a while. I kept thinking about Sol and her new life.

"Is she going to leave the AC on all day?" I asked.

"Huh?"

"For the souvenirs, so they stay purple", I explained.

"Ah. I don't know. Electricity is really expensive here," she answered, lost in her thoughts.

There was some time before the bus left, and we didn't want to wait in the terminal. We thought about going to eat something to kill time, but while Romina was searching her phone for somewhere to have dinner, the idea of going to the casino occurred to me. Romina was into it. Because we were still hungry, we went to the convenience store next door to buy some hot dogs and potato chips. We were unsure whether we should enter through the side door, which was open, or order through the window, so Romina stood in line and I went in. At first, there seemed to be no one inside, but the girl with endless black hair and faded clothes, the one from the first day, appeared from behind the counter. I was speechless, unable to order. She smiled at me and asked me what I needed.

"Two hot dogs," I said with a shaky voice. While she was preparing them, her back turned to me, I asked, "Why haven't you ever asked to read my palm?"

She turned around.

She gave me the hot dogs and said, "I saw your palm the first day you came in here. *Gitanas* don't tell each other's fortunes," she said.

Instead of grabbing the hot dogs, I started looking at the palm of my hand, the marks on it, its lines. I didn't see anything particular or different from any other palm. As my vision began to blur, Romina entered the convenience store "You should have told me they'd already served you. I stood in line like an idiot, and the one at the window sent me inside," she said, annoyed.

I didn't answer her. I was still staring at my palm. Romina paid, grabbed the hot dogs, and left. I looked up, but the girl had disappeared behind the counter again.

We ate the hot dogs while walking. I was looking at the palm of my hand and losing chips along the way. Romina asked what was wrong with me. Why wasn't I talking, and why did I keep walking with my hand in front of my eyes?

"Do you see anything?" I said, showing her my hand.

"In your hand?" she asked, looking closely. "Did you cut yourself or something?"

"No, I didn't cut myself," I answered. "But this looks like a normal hand to you?"

"Yeah, it's a normal hand. You have a little mayonnaise on your finger, but that's normal too."

We finished eating the hot dogs right before entering the casino. We walked up the red carpeted stairs. The place was full of people, mostly old retirees. I didn't feel like playing anything, but Romina wanted to buy some chips to play roulette.

"I want to bet on the 15 for the pretty girl, 45 for wine, 71 for excrement, 91 for the toilet, 22 for the crazy man, 73 for the hospital, 93 for the lovers, and 64 for crying," she said.

"How do you know what each number means?" I wanted to know.

"Ah, my dad is addicted to football pools," she told me.

"But is it the same meaning in roulette?" I asked, confused.

"Well, numbers are numbers. They're the same everywhere,"she answered.

"Ah, go figure. I didn't know."

We went to buy the chips, and Romina asked me if I had any change. I looked in my wallet and saw the little golden horseshoe. It was supposed to bring luck, and I thought it was a good idea for Romina to have it while playing. I gave her the change first then tried to remove the horseshoe that was compressed in that part of the wallet. When I managed to take it out, I realized that the tabs of acid were no longer there. I kept digging, but they were gone.

"Hey, I can't find the acid," I told Romina while I continued to search in every nook and cranny of the wallet.

But she wasn't listening. She was already walking toward the roulette table. I followed her, obsessed with the idea that the acid had disappeared.

Romina was disappointed when she reached the roulette table. It only had thirty-six numbers, so she could only bet on the pretty girl and the crazy man. She inverted the numbers for excrement and the toilet, leaving her with 17 and 19, which were misfortune and the fish. She wasn't entirely convinced, but she figured they sort of represented our trip to Mar del Plata. Because they were still greater than 36 when their digits were reversed, she added up the other numbers. The wine and crying became a stream, the hospital became milk, and the lovers became the soldier.

An older lady who heard her doing her number metamorphosis had gotten quite close to her, and when Romina finished making the bet, she told her, "Honey, I love your method."

"Thank you, ma'am," she replied with a proud smile.

Everyone was placing their bets. There was a constant bustle, but the sound that was most dominant was the noise of slot machines all mixed together, without synchronization. I was overwhelmed. There was too much noise and too many people in an enclosed space. Romina was focused on the game, and a bunch of old ladies gathered round, cheering her on. I had to get some fresh air. As I navigated between the machines, the poker tables, and the roulette wheels, I tried to remember if I had ever taken the acid out of the wallet. The last time I'd seen them had been in the cafe before buying the wine. Vague images from later that night appeared to me, but none were very clear or precise. I reached one of the exits and found myself outside on the boardwalk. It was already night, and the beach was dark. The sea reflected the moon. It looked like liquid silver, and I felt cozy and cool, like gazing out at a snowy mountain through the window of a warm cabin. I stared at it for a few minutes, then closed my eyes. I took a deep breath. When I opened them, I could swear I saw it: a black horse galloping, all alone, along the beach.

Marina Caamaño was born in 1980 in Buenos Aires, Argentina. For the past eight years, she has been living with six cats on an island off the coast of Brazil.

OTHER VERY FINE TITLES FROM
TRIDENT PRESS

Blood-Soaked Buddha/Hard Earth Pascal
by Noah Cicero

Tendrel: A Meeting of Minds
by Anne Waldman

Major Diamonds Nights & Knives
by Katie Foster

Cactus
by Nathaniel Kennon Perkins

The Pocket Emma Goldman

Sixty Tattoos I Secretly Gave Myself at Work
by Tanner Ballengee

The Pocket Peter Kropotkin

The Silence is the Noise
by Bart Schaneman

The Pocket Aleister Crowley

Propaganda of the Deed:
The Pocket Alexander Berkman

Echo Chamber
by Claire Hopple

What You Don't Expect from Me
by Matias Guillan

The Pocket Austin Osman Spare

America at Play
by Mathias Svalina

With a Difference
by Francis Daulerio and Nick Gregorio

Western Erotica Ho
by Bram Riddlebarger

Las Vegas Bootlegger
by Noah Cicero

The Green and the Gold
by Bart Schaneman

Selftitled
by Nicole Morning

The Only Living Girl in Chicago
by Mallory Smart

Tourorist
by Tanner Ballengee

Until the Red Swallows It All
by Mason Parker

Dead Mediums
by Dan Leach

Let's Walk Together
by Elva Ambía Rebatta & the Quechua Collective of NY

www.tridentcafe.com/trident-press-titles

www.ingramcontent.com/pod-product-compliance
Lightning Source LLC
Chambersburg PA
CBHW021720190726
48289CB00008B/2623